A Taste of Freedom

A story of the forgotten slave soldiers of the Civil War

Tommie Thompson (signature)

by

Tommie Thompson

ISBN: 1-4140-6179-X (e-book)
ISBN: 1-4140-6178-1 (Paperback)

Library of Congress Control Number: 2004090865

This book is printed on acid free paper.

Printed in the United States of America
Bloomington, IN

1st Books - rev. 03/05/04

Dedicated to the Confederate black soldiers
who fought in America's Civil War

As a nation we publicly honor our Civil War heroes, both North and South. However, there is never mention of the forgotten black soldiers. Surely their blood ran just as red when they shed it fighting for what they believed to be a just cause.

Some might argue that these soldiers were made to fight against their will or simply fought out of ignorance. Even if this line of thinking has merit, does this make them unworthy of mention? Are we simply to write them off as misguided traitors to their race in order to protect the reputations of those (past and present) who have conspired to keep this knowledge from the general public?

Is it possible that a number of slaves did not see themselves as being in bondage, but as members of a family unit, with a generational connection with their masters and the land?

Contrary to popular belief, some slaves were well treated by their masters, even to the point of regarding them as an extended family. Given these circumstances, they would not have considered Northern soldiers as liberators but as invaders who posed a threat to their families and their way of life. Therefore, they fought to protect what they held most sacred.

I, for one, refuse to ignore them or to judge them. My heart simply cries out to tell their story.

ACKNOWLEDGEMENTS

A special thanks to all those who encouraged me while writing my book and offered me much emotional support. I am especially indebted to my sister Barbara, who did not laugh (as most would!), when I first told her of my passionate desire to write this story. As she has always done, she challenged me to realize my dream. My soul mate and partner, Betty, allowed my thoughts to be in another place at times when they should have been of her. Tim Campbell, author of "All's Fair" encouraged me every step of the way. My editor, Jeanette Jennis, not only demanded, but would settle for nothing less but the very best from me, and never once pulled her punches! The Gulf Coast Writers Association accepted me into their fold, and provided unconditional support. And I will never forget all of the friends who believed in me, and those who offered to be my lab mice: Donna, Steve, Diana, Victoria, Elaine, Alice, Sandra, Dashila, Pam, and Jason. My gratitude knows no bounds!

CHAPTER ONE

Malachi looked at the children playing in the yard and glanced at his younger brother David who seemed to be having the time of his life. They knew nothing of the storm that was coming from the North, threatening their way of life. However, Malachi knew only too well because Master Bill had secretly taught him to read and write. Malachi was such a good student that he and Master Bill would read newspaper articles and have debates about current events, in private. They had become such good friends that Malachi was allowed to call him Bill when they were alone. Bill inherited the plantation when his father died of consumption five years earlier, and had much more liberal views when it came to slavery, but dare not let this become publicly known. If it came to a fight with the Yankees, his decision to do so would be based solely on the State's Rights issue and a firm resolve to protect the people he considered family, and his land. However, this would also give him the opportunity to let his slaves decide the course of their lives for themselves, making one of two choices: stay and fight for their home, or leave (with his blessings), to seek this illusive freedom that the Yankees were promising.

Malachi was deep in thought when he suddenly looked up and saw Bill walking up on the porch, with a look on his face that made Malachi's soul tremble. Bill opened his mouth to speak, but only silent despair came out. Finally, clearing his throat and calling Malachi by his nickname, he said, "Bubba, I must speak to you in private; I am afraid the time has come for us to prepare to face our worst fears. Please go to the house and wait for me in the study. I'll be along shortly." As Bubba walked toward Bill's house, he became overwhelmed with emotion; the kind of emotion that you feel when you have a dream that someone you love very much has died, and the pain that you feel from that loss is so great that your own sobbing awakens you.

Memories of years gone by seemed to flood his mind. He was remembering how he and Bill (as boys) would sneak into the kitchen and steal hoecakes. They had discovered that the cook took a break every day just before noon, and they took that opportunity to raid the kitchen. It was really great when they would find hot fried chicken on the stove, until one day the cook came back early. She entered the kitchen just as Bubba grabbed a hot chicken leg from the pan, shouting, "What are you boys doing in my kitchen?" Fortunately for Bubba, when she entered the kitchen his back was facing her, and out of pure fear upon hearing her voice, he shoved the hot chicken leg down the inside front of his pants. Needless to say, it took only a split second to find himself in a bad situation. That hot grease was cooking more than chicken! The cook never did get an answer because suddenly Bubba took off running out the back door, jumped off the porch, and just kept on running at breakneck speed. Bill had never seen anyone run so fast.

Bubba was headed for the creek, just a short distance away. When he finally reached it, he jumped in feet first. Bill, running close behind shouted, "Bubba, why did you take off running like the house was on fire, and jump into the creek with your clothes on?" Bubba put his hand Inside his wet pants and pulled out the chicken leg. He remembered how Bill laughed so hard that tears were streaming down his face. That incident quickly put an end to their kitchen raiding days.

As Bubba approached the big house, he paused for a moment, to drink in the sight of the beautiful home that stood before him. It was as if he were seeing it for the first time. The house looked so inviting, the splendor of it, almost took his breath away. Yes, this wonderful home, bright white with black shutters on each window and tall pillars gracing the front porch, was a delight to behold. Sometimes he felt that if he listened very carefully, he could almost hear the rustling leaves on the Oak trees that lined both sides of the path leading to the house, saying, "Come on in, you're welcome here."

He opened the front door and could see his reflection in the mirror-like, highly polished oak floors. He looked up at the beautiful chandelier suspended from the ceiling in all its glimmering glory. The winding, brilliant white staircase, leading upstairs to the massive bedrooms, was a work of art. He recalled how he and Bill (though reprimanded when caught), did their part to keep the oak banister polished by sliding down it, when they figured no one was watching. He entered the parlor with its comfortable stuffed sofas and imported rugs, which complemented the polished floors. The painting of Bill's parents that hung over the gorgeous marble mantlepiece above the fireplace was so lifelike, it always made him feel as if they were watching his every move. He walked into the dining room, and thought about the opulent meals that had been served there, imagining the guests sitting at the huge table, darkly stained and polished to perfection, laughing and talking about everything under the sun. Bubba shuddered as he began to visualize this magnificent home being destroyed by the

Yankees. He quickly put that unhappy picture out of his mind and continued on his way.

When Bubba entered the study, he sat in the chair that he had occupied so many times before, and began to ponder the fact that he had never raised his hand in anger to anyone, let alone a white man. Just the thought of doing so made him feel sick to his stomach. He was trying to decide if this sick feeling was coming from a fear of taking another man's life, or a fear of putting his own life in jeopardy in order to do so. He finally came to the conclusion that no man knows whether or not he is capable of killing until he comes face-to-face with that decision. Bubba sensed that he would soon have a chance to meet his own "moment of truth" because the look on Bill's face told him that America's Civil War had begun.

After speaking with Bubba, Bill felt he needed time to reflect for a short while. He had attended a meeting along with all the other plantation owners in the area the previous week. It was decided that when the first shot of the pending war was fired, a call to arms would be sounded. That call had come in the form of a rider on horseback this very morning, spreading the news that Southern soldiers had fired on Fort Sumter. He never dreamed that the first shot of the war would be fired in his home state of South Carolina. He felt anger swelling inside of him as he imagined the lovely town of Folsom and its surrounding plantations invaded by Yankee soldiers. Bill recalled the odd yet familiar feeling that came over him this morning when he saw the rider approaching. He thought it strange that the man was dressed completely in black, and riding a magnificent black stallion, moving at a slow gallop. Bill suddenly remembered why this unnerved him. As a boy, his father had taken him to an art museum on a visit to New York where he had seen a similar scene in a painting depicting the Angel of Death. Ever since, Bill had been periodically plagued by dreams of that scene.

Wandering the grounds for some time now, Bill figured he had better start toward the house. He had to share this grim news with Bubba, and together they must decide how best to tell the more than 200 slaves living on the plantation how the course of their lives was about to be changed forever.

As Bill walked into the study, he saw Bubba sitting there in that big stuffed chair that he loved so much, looking as if he had the weight of the world on his shoulders. Then, something hit him like a lightning bolt. He had traveled the country and gone to Europe several times. Bubba, on the other hand, (except for an occasional trip to Folsom), had never set foot off the plantation grounds. He had been such an excellent student that just holding a conversation with him on any topic would give anyone the impression that he was a world traveler. But, in fact, plantation life was the only world he truly knew.

Looking at Bubba, Bill remembered how they first met. It was when his mother (who was the housekeeper at the time), started bringing Bubba along to help with the chores. Bill had never been allowed to play with any of the slave children, so this presented an opportunity to satisfy his curiosity. He wondered what these people thought about when they were not working, what kind of games they played, and above all, how they truly felt about being slaves. He got his chance the very next morning. As soon as Bill's father left to attend to his duties on the plantation, he made it a point to be at the back door when the housekeeper appeared with her son. When Alice entered the room, Bill was standing there with a very mischievous look on his face, wanting to be recognized. Alice reluctantly introduced Bill to Bubba, thinking, Lord, what is this child up to now, as she began her chores. The two of them just stood there looking at each other for what seemed like a full minute. Bubba wondered why this blonde, fair-skinned white boy, kept staring at him and grinning. At that moment, Bill decided that this little light-skinned boy, with the proud look in his alert brown eyes, could become his friend. Upon closer inspection, it became clear to Bill that Bubba was somewhat afraid, but hiding it well. After all, he had never been this close to the Master's son, let alone spoken to him. Bill calmed his fear, asking him, "Do you want to see my room?" Bubba, eyes big, said, "I have to help my mama with her chores." Bill thought quickly and replied, "I'll tell your mother to excuse you from your chores today." Bubba looked at his mama and she nodded that he could go. As they entered Bill's room Bubba looked utterly amazed. This was a far cry from the small room that he and his two brothers, David and Jab, shared in his family's cabin.

Bill watched as Bubba glanced around the room, noticing that his eyes kept coming back to the bookshelf. "How old are you, Bubba?" "I be fohteen years old come Satiday." Grabbing Bubba by the shoulders, Bill started laughing gleefully, shouting, "That's my birthday too and I'll be fourteen, just like you!" This news made Bubba laugh too. Bill saw the fear that he had sensed earlier melting away, and found himself being overcome with a strong feeling that they were somehow meant to be together. Maybe they both needed someone to depend on and confide in. Yes, in this slave boy Bill saw the making of a true friendship. When they had both settled down, Bill walked over to the bookshelf and selected a book of fairy tales. "Bubba, do you know anything about books?" "I ain't nevah even seen one til now, (though he had once overheard his mama speak of them in a whisper to his daddy) let lone know sometin bout them." Bill knew very well that it was forbidden to teach slaves how to read and so did Bubba. Bill began talking to Bubba about the wonderful stories that books contained, some true and some simply made up to entertain people. He opened the book and slowly began to read it aloud. Bubba was hanging on every word. After reading several pages he stopped abruptly. "Please don't stop, Master Bill." "I must stop Bubba! My father will be home soon to eat his mid-morning meal, and I'll be in big trouble if he catches you in my room. Don't worry Bubba, I'll find a way to continue reading to you, and perhaps, if you'd like, I'll teach you how to read. Only, Bubba, you must promise to tell no one, not even your family!" "I promise, Master Bill, I keep our secret." After Bubba left the room, Bill hoped that he had not made a promise that he would live to regret.

CHAPTER TWO

Bill had to think of how to keep Bubba close to him, in a way that his father would approve. As he left his room, he noticed Bernard (his father's manservant), coming up the stairs. Slowly, an idea began to take shape and he smiled to himself, just thinking about the possibilities. However, he knew that he must think this through very carefully before presenting this masterpiece of an idea to his father.

Bill knew that his father was actually a very kind man. He also knew that he loved him very much and always did what he thought was in Bill's best interest. Since the loss of his mother two years earlier, his father had become a bit overly protective. Scarlet fever took its toll on a lot of families the same year his mother died of it. He thought of her often and sometimes longed for that feeling of security that her warm embrace gave him. It really made him feel very close to her when someone would point out how much he looked like his mother. They would say that he had her fair skin, the same blue eyes and that curly blonde hair which she seemed never to be able to control. He felt as if she was living on through him. This made the pain of her death a little more bearable, and he knew that he must live his life in such a way that she would always be proud of him.

Bill had never seen his father commit an act of cruelty toward any of the slaves. He was, however, very strict on tradition. That meant keeping them in their place by never doing anything through action, word or deed to allow them to think that they were anything other than slaves. So, with this thought in mind, Bill decided that he would approach his father with his idea at suppertime.

During supper they both made small talk; his father telling him how great the fields looked, and he in turn telling him about his day, being careful not to mention his encounter with Bubba. His father seemed to be in a rather good mood that night, so like any normal teenager, he decided that now was the time to strike. However, he was taken totally by surprise when his father suddenly asked him what he wanted for his birthday. Bill put his hand to his chin and began rubbing it as if he were giving this question a great deal of thought. Finally, he said, "Father I shall turn fourteen next Saturday and I've been thinking that soon I will be a full-grown man. I should start learning how to run the plantation and have more contact with the slaves, so that they will have greater respect for me as the Master's son and do my bidding as if you, yourself, were speaking." Bill's father gave him a look of wonder and pride, and thought to himself that what his son said was very true. After all, he would be taking over the responsibilities of this plantation one day, and he wanted him to be fully prepared when the time came. Bill could tell by the look in his father's eyes that he had struck pay dirt and he was determined to strike while the iron was hot. He quickly continued without giving his father a chance to reply. "I should like to start in a small way for now, and expand my authority as I gain the knowledge required to supervise slaves. Bernard has been your manservant for as long as I can remember. He performs his duties as if he were born to it, seeing to your every need, most times without even being told what those needs are. I have decided that a manservant is what I truly desire for my birthday present. Although I have in mind a much younger version of Bernard, someone that I will train to meet my needs and be my eyes and ears among the slaves. You have taught me that one must earn loyalty and respect, and I promise you, father, that I shall rise to the occasion."

Bill's father was thinking that if the plantation ever failed to provide a proper living for his son, surely he would make an excellent lawyer. Bernard has been a devoted slave and if he would let it be known, also a true friend and confidant. He dare not share with his son the fact that he had secretly taught Bernard how to read and write, and that he regarded him as much more than a mere servant. True friendship and loyalty were hard to come by in his world, and Bernard had become someone with whom he could share his most intimate feelings and emotions. As a plantation owner he was constantly gone, either taking care of the plantation or away on business, and he knew that Bill was lonely. Granting his request and letting him get more involved in dealing with the slaves would help to ease the guilt that he often felt when he had to be away from his son so much.

"So, what is your answer father? Am I to be granted my birthday wish?" "Bill, you are the type of son that any man could be proud of, so I will grant your request. However, the slave that you choose must meet my approval. Do you have any particular one in mind?" His father's rapid answer again took him by surprise; he could not believe his good fortune. "As you know, father, the housekeeper brings her son every day to help her with the chores. He appears to be a very hard worker and seems to know his place. He has good manners, is well groomed and with proper training, I think he would serve me well." Bill did not notice his father's face turning somewhat pale. His father knew very well the slave boy his son spoke of, and he wondered why the terrible deeds a person commits in the dark, always seem to come back to haunt him. He certainly felt haunted in that moment, as painful memories engulfed him.

His wife had a very difficult time during her pregnancy, so he had turned to a pretty slave girl for sexual comfort. Yes, he knew this slave boy very well indeed, because he was his illegitimate son. He found it ironic that the boy had been born premature and was delivered on the same day as his son, Bill. In order to cover up his indiscretion, he removed Alice from her other duties on the same day he found out that she was with child, and a short time later brought her into his home as housekeeper. He then approached a trusted slave named Louie and made him a proposition. This was one of the rare occasions when he wanted a slave to do something of his own free will. So Louie agreed to take Alice as his wife and raise the child as his own. In exchange for this favor, he would be given a job in the horse stables, much easier work than tending the fields, and he would also have a new cabin built to accommodate this newfound family. Louie had always been secretly in love with Alice, but the ten-year difference in their ages had always stopped him from approaching her; this was like a gift from God. Alice and Louie were both sworn to secrecy concerning this whole incident, coupled with a threat that they could both be sold to another plantation owner, if they ever talked to anyone about this matter. They both knew that Master James would do anything to prevent his wife from having to bear the shame of his affair with a slave girl. Satisfied that he had sufficiently covered his tracks, he promised himself that he would never be unfaithful again. He loved his wife very much and his heart ached at the thought of her ever finding out about his infidelity.

James considered himself a religious man, and so thinking along those lines, he contemplated the possibility of some divine force at work here. Wasn't it odd that of all the slave boys on the plantation his son should choose this one? Was this God's way of punishing him for his past indiscretion? Or was this His way of making things right? He decided that whatever the case might be, he was not going to interfere. His conscience over the years had caused him too many sleepless nights; perhaps his son unknowingly could help him to fulfill the obligation he felt deep inside his very soul toward Bill's brother.

Bill sat patiently waiting for his father's answer, silently praying that he would approve of Bubba. After what seemed to be hours, his father spoke. "I'm quite familiar with Alice's son and everything you say about him is true. Therefore, I approve of your choice and have no doubt that he will make an excellent manservant." Bill leapt from his seat and hugged his father so hard that he turned red. It had been a long time since he had seen such a look of joy on his son's face. It was decided that Bubba would start training for his new duties the very next morning, and they both knew that Alice would be happy about her son's new status.

After bidding his father goodnight, Bill retired to his room to contemplate just how he would go about training Bubba. He decided that first he must furnish him with some new clothes; after all he could not have his manservant looking like a field hand. He would also fulfill his promise and teach him how to read and write. He knew that after a time it would become rather boring trying to communicate with someone who was illiterate. This way Bubba could teach him about the world he knew, and Bill in turn would open up new worlds for him.

Bill went to sleep feeling really good about the events of the day, knowing that his whole life had changed in just a matter of hours, for the better. This was truly a turning point in his life. He hoped to deserve his father's trust that he would not only be an excellent master one-day, but also make a special, loyal friend of Bubba.

CHAPTER THREE

The years had been kind to both of them. Bill had learned much more than he bargained for from Bubba. He now took pride in treating his slaves with respect and as individuals, rather than as a mass of sub-humans simply brought here to do his bidding. Bubba was truly grateful to Bill for exposing his mind to the vast world that existed outside of the plantation. However, his heart was here and he was content to be surrounded by the land and the people he loved. They would soon reach their twenty-fifth birthdays, but there was little cause for celebration because of the imminent danger that loomed over the plantation.

Bill did not waste time with small talk; he shared the information he had received from the messenger that morning. Bubba looked him straight in the eye and said, "Bill, I believe that defending our home is the right thing to do, but I must admit that I am scared to death, and we've been friends long enough for me to realize that you are, too. I also know that our belief in God and the strength of our unwavering friendship will give us the courage to face and do the horrible things that will be required of us, and also allow us to accept the loss of friends and loved ones who will surely die in this effort." It was decided that if it came to war with the Yankees, that together they would tell the others living on the plantation everything that would be at stake (including their lives). They would then be better prepared to make a wise decision.

In anticipation of war, the Confederate States had been supplying extra rifles to their militia units for several months. The idea was to have a properly trained force of men on the home front, if needed.

Gun handling wasn't new to Bill or Bubba, since whenever Bill went hunting as a young boy, he would take Bubba with him. He decided that since he showed such a zest for learning new things that he would teach Bubba how to shoot. Eventually, as with everything else, he became an expert shot. Just how good was proven to him on one particular trip. They were walking in the woods looking for game, when he turned to Bubba and asked him to wait for a moment while he looked for a place to relieve himself. Bubba had been waiting what seemed a long time, so he started off in the direction Bill took, and finally found Bill squatting down with his pants below his knees (bare ass showing), looking as white as a sheet. Bubba followed Bill's eyes to the problem. About one foot from his ass there was a rattlesnake poised to strike; Bubba quickly raised his rifle and fired, blowing the snake's head clean off. Bill, with a crazy look on his face, mumbled "thanks", then fainted dead away. Bubba shook Bill back to consciousness. When Bill looked up and saw Bubba leaning over him he grabbed and hugged him for dear life, saying, "Bubba, you have saved me from a most embarrassing death." Bubba looking over his shoulder, quickly replied, "No, my friend, because if someone should see you hugging me like this with your pants down, it would be the death of both of us." Bill suddenly had a picture in his mind of how this would look to a passerby, and he laughed. Oh, how he laughed! Bubba joined in saying, "Promise that you won't think of me every time you take a crap." This evoked more howls of laughter from both of them. When Bill stood up and began to pull up his pants, Bubba could not help but notice a red birthmark that resembled a strawberry on his right leg. He found this very odd, because he had a similar birthmark in the exact same place. He smiled to himself and figured his eyes must be playing tricks on him, thinking, next thing I know, I'll be seeing the ghost of the dead snake.

Bubba, with his knowledge of guns, had secretly taught select slaves how to use them. They never imagined that one day they would be asked to use them for the purpose of killing men. It was all part of the plan that he and Bill had put together for the defense of the plantation. These were men that he felt would stand beside him to protect this land that they, too, loved.

At the plantation and landowners' meeting Bill said that he would accept a commission of Captain in the Confederate Militia, provided that his command would consist mainly of his loyal slaves and any volunteers, black or white, who would be willing to fight and die side by side in the protection of Folsom and its surrounding communities. Cries of indignation and laughter came swiftly from the other landowners. Bill knew that in order to gain their support for his plan, he had to figure out a way to use their bigoted attitudes to his advantage.

He went on to explain the logic in his plan, shouting at times in order to be heard. "Gentlemen, capable white men such as yourselves will be desperately needed throughout the South if we are to win this war against the North. Most of you have already indicated that you will serve as officers in the regular army, and that it is your desire to take the fight to the enemy. Doing this will leave your loved ones and plantations with minimal protection, given the fact that a good many citizens and militiamen will be going with you." Bill paused before continuing, "I ask you to just think for a moment, gentlemen. We all have slaves that are and have been fiercely loyal to us. We have trained them to nurse and help raise our children and cater to our every need. They look upon our loved ones as their own family; most of them would give their very lives to protect them. Gentlemen, if we muster our loyal male slaves and give them proper training, naturally with a white man giving the orders, we would have a formidable force to stop the Yankees from violating that which we hold dear."

When Bill finished speaking, there was dead silence in the room. The laughter and cries of indignation, which had filled the room moments earlier, were replaced with applause and praise. The chairman of the Landowners Association came over and put his arm around Bill while saying, "This plan to turn our slaves against the very men that intend to free them, is a stroke of genius. I am sure that I speak for everyone here when I say that if it comes to war, we will give you everything you need to accomplish your mission; it is indeed an honor to have such a fine patriot to the Confederate cause among us."

Bill's mind returned to Bubba's dilemma. "I, too, have misgivings about putting men's lives on the line, but I've never heard of a war where people didn't die. We all have to be prepared to make the ultimate sacrifice. This won't be a game that ends with everyone getting up and going home when it's over. The comfort comes from knowing that they will have died fighting for what they believe to be right. This is why it is imperative that every man who joins us understands exactly what he's getting himself into."

"Bill, tomorrow will be a hard day for both of us. I suggest we get a good night's sleep, as we will need all of our wits about us. There is little we can plan until we know exactly how many slaves will stand with us." Bill agreed and suggested that they call all of the people living on the plantation together before they went to the fields in the morning, and share the news with them; for some it would be tragic and others (he had no doubt), would see this as an opportunity to escape into the arms of the Yankees, and freedom. "Bubba, I really don't know what I will say to them; asking men to kill and possibly be killed for this land is a difficult task. However, I do know that my words must be sincere and come straight from the heart." They both said goodnight and parted, each man deep in his own thoughts.

CHAPTER FOUR

While walking back to his cabin, Bubba thought about how all these years he played the role of an illiterate slave, conversing literately only when he was alone with Bill. It had been very difficult not to give his educated opinion when certain topics would come up among a few of the other slaves, especially topics concerning freedom. Little did they know that freedom came with a price that they were not capable of paying at this point in time. They gave little thought to the fact that they were not responsible for anything but doing what they were told to do. He wished he could tell them that although slavery is wrong in every sense of the word, the consequences of instant freedom for an unprepared people would be disastrous. Bubba thought, this is what it might feel like: You go to bed a slave and you wake up the next morning a free man. With the realization of this, you start jumping up and down and shouting for joy! Suddenly, you also realize that now you can pack your things and go out into the world. You fall to your knees and thank Jesus for the wonderful blessing he has given you. But tell me brother; is this really a blessing from Jesus, or maybe the work of the Devil himself? The world that you are so eager to be part of is full of merciless pitfalls.

Bubba's reflection on the past had unwittingly led him to the present; he now knew exactly what he must tell his fellow slaves in the morning. He would speak to them in a language they could understand. If they ever found out that he could talk and think logically like a white man, his friends would feel betrayed, thinking he had been making fools of them. He would be classified as an "upper class lackey" and be shunned by them. His relationship with his fellow slaves had been wonderful so far. He had been looked upon as a leader and a friend; someone to be counted on in times of need, and this is the way it must be kept.

The time had come to break the promise he made to Bill (he knew in his heart that Bill would understand), and tell his parents the truth about his capabilities. Bubba did not want to die or lose his parents in the coming conflict without them knowing about his accomplishments. They would be very proud of him. He would tell them tonight. He had no doubts about his secret being safe with them. However, he decided not to tell his brothers or his sister, Bee. David and Jab would get drunk on any given night (not that he was opposed to taking a drink now and then himself), and let it slip; Bee would also eventually tell her boyfriend, George. He loved his siblings but that did not mean he had to give up his common sense to prove it.

As he approached the cabin he knew that his siblings would still be out gallivanting or courting, giving him the opportunity to speak freely to his parents. As usual, they were sitting on the porch when he walked up, enjoying the night air, although his daddy seemed to be enjoying it a little too much, with the cup of home brew by his chair. He leaned over and kissed his mama while saying (in perfect English), "I trust you and father have had a splendid day and are ready to face tomorrow with the utmost enthusiasm." She looked at him as if he were a stranger and thought to herself, this boy done got drunk and lost his mind; he left here this afternoon a black man and he come back talkin like a white man, spoutin words I don't even know what they mean. Bubba could not help but laugh at the expressions on their faces. Before either one could respond, he asked them to come into the privacy of the cabin where he would explain everything to them.

Bubba and his parents seated themselves at the kitchen table, a great place for family conversation. Alice asked him, "You been drinkin, son?" He quickly replied, "No, mama, I have not been drinking and I definitely have not lost my mind, if that was going to be your next question. I have something to tell both of you that I have been keeping a secret for a long time because of a promise I made to Master Bill.

Mama, do you remember when you used to take me to the big house to help you with the chores when I was just a boy, and one day Master Bill told you to excuse me from work so he could show me his room?" "I show do son, I remember that well, you was a good little worker. I recall thinkin at the time, just what was that little brat up to now? But turned out, it was the best thang that evah happened to you." "Funny you should say that mama, because as it turns out, you are sure right." His daddy, (having been silent all this time), suddenly said, "What do you mean, son, has somethin good happened today?" "No, daddy, something wonderful came about when I entered that room long ago. Bill took a liking to me right off. I'm allowed to call him by his given name when we are alone. When we found out that we have the same birth date, it somehow made our meeting real special."

Alice's heart started racing; she was gripped with fear thinkin that Bubba had found out that Bill was his brother. If she could have taken back those times she slept with the Master she surely would, but it wasn't her decision to make. She was then and still is, just a slave, here to do her Master's biddin. She would nevah forgit that day. It seemed that the sun had no mercy on the field hands; sweat was runnin down her body like water. She felt faint, wishin she could get to some shade for just a few minutes, but knowin all along that it would be dinner time befoe she could enjoy the welcomed shade of her cabin, if only for a little while.

The master had been to the fields twice that day, and more than once she felt his eyes on her. Although she had nevah been with a man, she knew that look that a man gives a woman when he's thinkin with the wrong head. She knew that the male slaves considered her to be a pretty young thang, but the older women were always protectin her from them. Whenever men would come sniffin round they would say, "Ya'll go way now, cause ya'll ain't gone git nothin here, this brown sugar is savin her goodies for a husband." As a young girl, she new very little bout sex, but from time to time she would hear talk bout how the Master's wife was doin poorly and maybe not fulfillin her womanly duties toward him. The older women said that it wouldn't be long befoe he'd be lookin for a pretty sweet slave girl to stick his poker in. She remembered she used to laugh to herself when she heard them say that. Although only eighteen, she knew what that meant. She also recalled how on that hot, sweaty day he came to their cabin right aftah dinnertime; her parents had already headed back to the fields. Knowin their daughter was not feelin well, they told her to stay in the cabin for a bit and sponge her body off with some cool water. They would make an excuse if Master James missed her.

Alice quickly took her clothes off, stepped into a wooden tub of refreshin water and began to sponge her body. She could feel her body start to cool down nicely when suddenly she heard the cabin door open. Thinkin it was one of her parents comin back to fetch somethin, she was slow to react to the sound. When she did glance at the door there stood the Master, lookin at her body as if it were a piece of cake. She knew now that the women on the plantation had been right. The Master had chosen her.

After he had his way with her, he swore her to silence by threatenin to sell her parents to the neighborin plantation owner who was known to be harsh and cruel to his slaves. She thought, ain't it funny how slaves had a way of measurin the harshness and cruelty that was put upon them. She knew what the Master did to her was wrong, but he had been gentle with her and seemed almost embarrassed, his manly needs too strong to control. He needed a woman, and deep inside herself she felt somewhat flattered that he had chosen her.

After that, life became much easier for her and her family. Her father gave thanks to God when one day the Master came up to him and said that he and his family were loyal slaves and good workers, and as a reward, he and his family would be removed from the fields and given easier tasks. Alice knew what her main job would be, but she didn't mind cause it was savin her parents from a lifetime of backbreakin work, pickin cotton, and gettin old befoe they time. There was much joy in their cabin that night. She didn't recall evah seein her parents so happy.

She never once thought about gettin pregnant, her period didn't come for two months straight. Goin to her mama with this news would force her to tell all that was goin on between her and the Master. Even knowin that her mama had seen these thangs happen many times befoe in other slave families, she knew that her parents would be deeply hurt. She decided that there was no one to share her shame with, except the Master.

When she told him of her plight, she could see he was not only angry and upset, but also quite scared, though he tried to hide it from her. There was no doubt that if they were found out, his marriage would be in trouble. A few days later he came to her with a plan that he felt would protect them both. Naturally, she had no say in the matter. After all that love makin, she was still just a slave and had to do her Master's biddin. She was to be put to work in the big house as a housekeeper. This move would allow him to make life easier for her and the unborn child without drawin suspicion. He also explained the arrangements he had already worked out with Louie.

In a short period of time she had gone from bein a virgin to sleepin with the Master, and now she was to marry a man she didn't love. She thought to herself, how wonderful it would be if a slave could make her own choices in life, but took comfort in the thought that maybe someday her child would be able to do so. She knew that Louie was a kind and decent man, and she was well aware that he had always been in love with her. He was a fun-lovin person, and Louie always looked at the bright side of thangs. Most folks round the plantation couldn't rightly go through the day without hearin one of the jokes he was always tellin. That man could make anybody laugh, even if they didn't have a mind to. Alice couldn't recall evah seein that short little notty head man when he didn't have a smile on his shiny black face, or a twinkle in those dark brown eyes. Still, she knew that underneath all that laughter was a very shy man, who could nevah drum up the courage to approach her. Maybe with time, she would grow to love him.

They would have to put on a show for the benefit of her parents, pretendin that they had been secretly courtin for some time. Gainin her parent's approval of the marriage would not be a problem; they, too, respected Louie for being a good man and a hard worker.

After the marriage, life went on as if nothin evah happened between her and the Master. Louie never once mentioned it or gave any sign that he evah thought bout it. When the baby was born prematurely months later, he was the proudest father that you evah did see. Lookin at the joy on his face when he held this baby boy made her realize that she and her child would be loved and cherished by this man, and that made her feel warm all over. If there was evah a man she could love, it surely would be this one. She found it strange that the Master's wife had her a baby boy on the same night she gave birth to Bubba. The Lord sure was workin in mysterious ways; it was as if there was some kind of plan in the makin.

Alice turned her attention back to Bubba. "Bubba, what's this wonderful news all bout?" "Ya'll wait right here, I have to get something out of my room." Bubba went to his shared bedroom and retrieved a book from his hiding place, a book Bill had given him to read when he was alone. He returned to the kitchen and put it on the table. Bubba had never seen such a look of fear on the faces of his parents; they looked at the book as if they were seeing the devil himself. Louie knew that Alice, (because of workin in the Big house), had seen books befoe and would tell him of how she loved to dust them off, when her chores called for her to be in the Master's library. She had told him that she truly believed that the words in those books gave the white man some kind of power over slaves, which is why it was forbidden to teach a slave to read and write. Louie recalled havin heard bout a slave on a neighborin plantation who was caught tryin to steal a book from his Master's house. News traveled fast mong the slaves, especially bad news. They beat that boy so bad his own mama couldn't recognize him. The only reason they didn't hang him was cause he was worth too much money to his Master. Louie shuddered at the thought of this happenin to his son; the boy he had taken as his own and truly loved.

Seeing how upset his parents had become, Bubba assured them that he had not stolen the book and that Bill had given it to him. Alice, with a look of relief on her face, asked, "Why would Master Bill do such a thang, knowin that you can't read?" Bubba gave his mama a warm smile. "That's just it mama, I can read and write, just as good as any white man. That is the news I have been longing to share with you and daddy for years. I really feel bad about not telling you before now, but as I told you, Bill made me promise that I would never tell anyone. He started teaching me soon after I became his manservant. Although we both knew that it was against the law to do this, the decision was made to teach each other about our different worlds. The only way I could learn about the white man's world was through an education, and he taught me well. I've had to play the fool these many years, but believe me when I say that I have not been playing you and daddy for fools. Telling you the truth would have caused you to live in fear of someone finding out and shouting it all over the plantation. Not telling you was my way of protecting you, because I love you both so very much."

Bubba picked up the book of poems and began to read to his parents. After reading several poems he looked up at his parents. There were tears of pride and joy streaming down his mama's face and his daddy seemed to be in shock. Bubba closed the book, then reached across the table and held the hands of his parents and said, "The day will soon come when any black person who chooses to, can learn to read and write without the fear of being beaten or hung for it." Stopping briefly to gain control of his emotions, and under the pretense of clearing his throat, Bubba continued, "As you already know, there have been rumors going around the plantation that say the white men from up North want the South to free the slaves and treat us as equals. I can now tell you that those rumors are true. The southern states have refused to be told what to do and how to run their lives by the Yankees and have left the Union. In the white man's world, this is called an act of civil disobedience. The Yankees say that there should be one set of rules to properly govern this nation, but the southern states don't see it that way. Now, I don't rightly know for sure but I think that the Yankees are more concerned about money than they are about freeing the slaves. A lot of plantation owners have gotten mighty rich, what with them having all this free labor to do their bidding. I also think that the Yankees are using us as an excuse to get want they really want, and you can count on it when I say it isn't a bunch of black folks running around the country singing spirituals and talking about their freedom. Now, I must tell you why I have picked this night to tell you the truth after so many years of keeping my secret. The so-called war to free the slaves has begun. Southern soldiers fired on Fort Sumter this very morning." With a look of desperation, Alice said, "Son, what will become of us if the soldiers come and make us leave the plantation? This is the only home we've evah known, most of us have nevah even been to Folsom! Are we to be just thrown out into the world?" Bubba reached across the table, and brushed the tears from his mama's face. "I have read the newspapers mama, which is a way the white men let each other know what's going on in the world. The Northerners are making promises that they say will help us adjust to this newfound freedom. I have a feeling deep inside that tells me when this war is over, and if the Yankees win it, those promises will be quickly forgotten and we will be left to provide for ourselves.

We all know that there are many slave masters who want to keep us in bondage forever, if they have their way. We also know that there are a few such as Bill, who treat us as family and with respect. This war just might give these men the chance to speak out and let their true feelings be known. I am not foolish enough to believe that they will speak out against the South, but I am hopeful enough that they will speak out for reform concerning slavery laws. Freedom will come much more slowly this way, but at least it will have a solid foundation, and we will have a chance to prepare ourselves for it. Daddy, you've always taught me that anything built without a solid foundation cannot stand the test of time; this I believe also to be true with people's lives."

Louie spoke, a grave look on his face. "It seem to me that we are in a fine mess. If the Yankees come here they will most likely kill the white folks, tell us that we is free, then make us leave the plantation; and as you say, not carin that we will have no place to go! If we refuse to leave, they just might take a mind to kill us, too." "Daddy, I don't care which way we turn, a great many people are going to die in this war! It matters not to the Angel of Death, whether they are Northerners or Southerners, nor what the color of their skin is. The souls of these brave men will stand before God, only He can judge who was right or wrong. When the killing is over, the only comfort they will leave their loved ones is that they died to protect them and the land they love. All a man can do is to stand up for what he believes in his heart to be right, and hope to God that he really is right." "Tell us son, what do you believe is the right thing to do?" Bubba could hear a slight tremble in his daddy's voice, as Louie continued talking. "We are proud that cause a yo books you have learned the ways of the white man's world, but still have your black common sense. I gotta say, you really had me worried when you first come home tonight. While you was talkin like a white man when you come up on the porch, I was sittin there tryin to figure out if the white folks have a special plantation they send black folks to when they goes crazy." Bubba and his mama burst out laughing. It took daddy to come up with something like that. Alice thought to herself, Lord I nevah seen nothin that could keep that man feelin low for long; he could find somethin funny in a graveyard.

As the laughter died down, Bubba's voice took on a serious tone. "Mama, I truly believe in the things I have told you and daddy tonight. Bill and I have known for months now that the slavery issue would soon lead to war with the North. We have put together a plan that will allow us to stay and protect this land." Louie, looking puzzled, shouted, "Tell me how ya'll figure that two men can protect this plantation from Yankee soldiers bent on killin!" "That's just it, daddy, it won't be just the two of us. The plantation owners and officials of Folsom have all agreed to form a militia that will be made up of both white and black soldiers." Louie looked hard at Bubba before saying, "I was right the first time, you really gone crazy and taken Master Bill with you!" "No, daddy, I am completely sane and so is Bill; this really is going to happen. Please! Just hear me out! The only reason those among them who are complete bigots agreed to it, was because Bill pointed out that while they are away (and taking most of the young men with them) seeking glory in battle, a militia should be formed to protect their loved ones and property. He also said to them, who better to be a part of this militia than the loyal slaves who have helped raise their families and would gladly lay down their lives to protect them. Of course, all of the officers will be white men. However, both races must learn to work together in order to form a good fighting unit. This is why the militia will be formed of only volunteers. Daddy, did you ever

37

think you would see the day when slaves and white men would come together for a common cause?" "Yeah son, I sure did, and somehow the word lynchin come to mind." Bubba looked at his father and shook his head. "Daddy, can't you be serious for a change?" "Bubba, I am bein serious. Cause soon as one of them slaves gits drunk and decide he gonna shoot him a white officer, that's what it gone be, a lynchin." "Daddy, I will admit that there is truth in what you say, but that's exactly why Bill or myself must approve all black volunteers; together we feel that we can weed out the hotheads that would be joining up just for the chance to get a rifle and kill white men. We will only take slaves that truly want to protect this land and their families, and who know from the start that they could be killed in the process, men who choose not to leave this land just because the Yankees say so! White men break promises to each other, so you know what they'll do to us." Bubba noticed the fear creeping into the eyes of his parents, as he continued to tell them of his and Bill's plan. "These men, white and black, will be fighting against this false freedom that will enslave our people even more, for years to come. These men who can be made to understand that the price of this freedom will be everlasting poverty for most of our people. These men who can see far enough to know that this would lead to depending on the Yankees for our very existence; which will mean that we will have to dance to their music whether we like it or not. These men will be men who are willing to take a chance that when this war is over (providing the South wins), that things will change for the better, and when freedom finally comes, they can stand up and be men who are prepared to take care of their families." In an attempt to provide some form of comfort, Bubba smiled at his parents, took his mama's hands, and held them gently, saying, "I guess when you really think about it, we slaves can't lose no matter who wins. Those of us who choose to fight for the South and live to tell about it, will be looked upon by the Yankees and some of our own people as lackeys or as having been forced to fight for the South by our Masters, and we'll be freed along with all the other slaves, and in time we will become forgotten soldiers. Mama, I decided to share all this news with you and daddy tonight because I felt that you should hear it directly from me, instead of along with everyone else who will be called together and told about it the first thing in the morning. Bill and I are determined to explain how we see this war and the choices our people will soon have to make."

Satisfied that his parents understood, Bubba said, "Well, my dear parents, I for one must get some sleep and so should you. Tomorrow will be a powerful day in all our lives; we will talk again after the meeting, but please remember that any decision you make could never change my love for you." As Bubba got up from the table he heard the cabin door open. He turned to see who it was, and in walked his brothers smelling like a whiskey still. David drunkenly asked, "What ya'll doin up so late?" Louie quickly replied. "Don't be worried bout what we doin up so late! Where's your sister? And don't tell me ya'll left her alone with George, cause he's a sly one, that boy. If she comes up pregnant I'm goin beat both ya'll ass for the whole nine months that she is." Their sister Bee entered the cabin, which was filled with laughter, and when they saw her coming through the door, they laughed even harder. She knew then that the joke was on her but she did not mind; she just silently thanked God for bein able to come home to a family that had such love for each other. They finally said their goodnights and went off to bed, with only Bubba and his parents knowing of the peril headed their way. For them, deep thought would truly be a bedfellow tonight.

CHAPTER FIVE

Sleep would give Bill no reprieve from the thoughts of doubt that began to plague him after Bubba left that evening; convincing these slaves to fight for this land would be a very difficult task. He knew that Bubba was the only man who could persuade them that this would be in their best interest in the long run. Finally, Bill realized that the outcome of tomorrow (with the help of his silver-tongued friend Bubba), would be in God's hands. With that thought, which brought him a measure of comfort, peaceful sleep finally came.

Bill awakened with a start, thinking he had slept late into the morning. He looked out the bedroom window and saw that it was still dark outside. He knew that Bubba would arrive early in order to give them enough time to have a discussion before meeting with the others and sharing what for some would be grim news, and for others a deliverance.

Bill had just finished enjoying his first cup of morning coffee when Bubba walked into the study. Bubba immediately began telling him that he had broken his promise and shared with his parents the fact that he was literate, but before he could explain why, Bill interrupted him saying, "Bubba, I understand completely and I forgive you; under the given circumstances, I probably would have done the same thing. These will be very trying times for all of us, so now is the time to unburden our hearts to those we love. I want you to know that not only have I regarded you as a true friend but also one that I could not love more, even if you were my own brother. I realize how difficult life has been for you these past years; it's been a hard thing to do, pretending to be ignorant except when we are alone. You have all this knowledge bursting to be let out, yet you've had to contain it. Trust me, my friend. I promise you that I will do everything in my power to hasten the day when not only you but also all black people will have the freedom to educate themselves without fear from any man." It was obvious to Bill that Bubba had been deeply moved because he turned his head to keep Bill from seeing the tears welling up in his eyes. However, Bill knew that this moment of sadness would soon turn to one of joy because of the information he was about to share with Bubba. He could hardly wait to see the look on Bubba's face.

"Bubba, you are well aware that to my knowledge, I have no living relatives. Realizing that there is a strong possibility that I could be killed in battle, I had my lawyer draw up some papers, which you will find, if and when the time comes, in a strongbox located in my bottom desk drawer. Those papers give you and your family your freedom and enough money to start and maintain a financially secure new life. The money is in gold coin; that way you are protected, no matter which side wins this war. You know my lawyer, Mr. Dwinn, very well, and you also know he is an honorable man and will do right by you. If you find yourself in need of his assistance in any way, do not hesitate to contact him. He and I have discussed the possible difficulties you would face, if I should die, and he is prepared and willing to help you on my behalf. This action will keep all of you from being bought and sold; only God knows what would happen to you. Although I know slave reform will eventually come about, I simply don't want to take any chances with your life; at least this way you'll have options. If you think I'm going to stop looking out for you just because I'm dead, you're in for a big surprise." Bubba did not laugh at Bill's attempt at humor; he just stood, as if frozen in place, looking quite dazed.

"Well, Bubba, aren't you going to say something?" "I don't know what to say, Bill! How can I possibly find the words to say how grateful I am, I am filled with mixed emotions. On one hand, the thought of being free, overwhelms me. I mean, just think. Me! Being free and rich!" He paused, taking a deep breath. "And thanks to you, I have enough intelligence to put that money to proper use. On the other hand, the thought of you having to die, in order for me to gain freedom and prosperity, is a terrible thing I would never wish for. I've always known in my heart, that you would eventually give me my freedom, and under normal circumstances, you also know, that I would never leave you, even though I'd be free to do so. However, if you should fall in battle, I will, with a heavy heart, honor your wishes. But, tell me, Bill, why have you avoided talking about the possibility of my being killed in battle? You see, my friend, just as I choose not to think of you lying dead on a battlefield, I am sure your mind refuses to visualize my life coming to such a tragic end." Walking to where Bill stood, Bubba placed his arm around his best friend, saying somberly, "Let's end this depressing conversation, because I truly believe that God has a long life planned for both of us." With that said, the two men sat down, suddenly lost in memories crowding out thoughts of death and war.

Bubba thought how unfortunate it was that Bill had no family. A lonely young boy had grown into a man who must often feel alone. Bubba found it ironic that such a man could understand the joy others felt being surrounded by loved ones, and be generous enough to give the best of what he had to offer, to others. How blessed Bubba felt to have such a friend!

Bill was thinking of how he kept from indulging in self-pity for all these years, especially after his father became seriously ill, right after his sixteenth birthday. For years he had gone to see numerous doctors, but even the most prominent of them were unable to cure his condition. Bill painfully remembered how his father, (who was a 6'2", 200 pound, handsome man), had become a mere shadow of himself, his health deteriorating to the point where he was completely bedridden. Bill was constantly at his bedside, and on the day of his death, he recalled how helpless he felt knowing that there was nothing he could do to save his beloved father. He clutched Bill's hand tightly as he called out his wife's name, as if she were standing there before him. As he took his last breath, a look of joy and contentment appeared on his face; and Bill knew instantly that his father was reunited with his mother, the woman he had never stopped loving. The memory of that scene gave him much comfort throughout the years. Although it had not been easy going through life with no family, somehow he managed to find the strength to do so by helping others. He took pleasure in doing good deeds for his slaves and neighbors alike. He often sensed that this intuitive compassion for others was passed down from his mother; his father's tendency was to meet his own needs first, and consider those of others after the fact.

Over the years Bill had many sexual encounters. Most of these ladies had sordid reputations, and the ones that did not, he had no desire to court, let alone marry. These days he went to Folsom once a week and slept with Mona, a prostitute that he'd singled out to keep for himself. She was a fine-looking woman and was eager to enter into a special arrangement with him. His thinking was that it would keep him from doing something foolish and permanent, out of sheer frustration, like marrying the wrong woman. Thus far, he was pretty content with the life he made for himself.

Bill knew that Bubba was sweet on a girl named Hattie, although he sometimes referred to her as "Hottie," because to hear him tell it, she sure set his soul on fire! Hattie was a very pretty girl; petite, with golden brown skin, short brown hair wonderfully matching it, and a look of innocence in her lovely brown eyes. She was the youngest of three sisters and four brothers and Bubba lacked the nerve to ask her parent's permission to court her; which meant they had to sneak around for fear of her parent's finding out. Bubba feared her mother far more then he did her father and brothers. He would say,

"That's the meanest woman I ever did see; it's a wonder any of them boys got any sense at all, seeing as how she done wore their heads out with that black frying pan. With that woman it's frying pan first and questions later. They took in a young man named Arthur, who had no family here. To keep things respectable, they told him that if he wished to remain with them he had to marry one of their daughters. He told them that he would have to think about it. Next thing I know he's getting married to Hattie's sister, Rosa. Funny thing is, I know for a fact that Arthur had no knot on his head when he entered that cabin, but on the day their mama announced there was going to be a wedding, Arthur was standing there pretty as you please with a knot on his head the size of a lemon. I think their mama introduced him to Mr. Frying Pan and that must have been a hell of a wallop because he still has that knot on his head to this day. Throughout the plantation they are known as good people; I must admit that there is a lot of love in that cabin, and they all seem to take their mama's strict rules in stride. Hattie and each of her siblings are as different as day and night; she's the adventurous type willing to take life head on and worry about the consequences later. I like that quality about her, but I'm also afraid that her overly zealous nature might come back to haunt her in later years. Even with their different personalities, the rest of them are pretty much easy going and hard working people. However,

I mean to marry this girl someday; she has the kind of vitality that inspires a man to accomplish things in life." The stories that Bubba would sometimes tell him about the humorous side of that family still made him smile.

He recalled the time Bubba told him about Hattie's mother almost catching them kissing down by the creek. He said, "She just appeared out of nowhere. You talk about being scared, my legs were shaking so bad I could not have run even if I had wanted to and believe you me, I wanted to. Hattie was as cool as a cucumber." She said, "Mama would you please come over here and help me get this trash out this man's eye, cause if he keep rubbin it the way he was when I walked up, he gone go blind in it." As her mother approached she pulled his eyelid wide open and blew into it; her mother looked at his eye and said, "He must have gotten some sand in it, child," and she in turn blew into it. "I played my part" and said, "That show feels better Ma'm, I don't mean to be no trouble." Hattie's mother said, "Isn't no trouble at all son, the trouble gone come if I find out you been messin round with my daughter." Bubba opened his mouth to speak, but before he could she had grabbed Hattie by the arm and was headed away from the creek; he wondered what would have happened if she had caught them kissing and shuddered at the thought.

Bill knew that Bubba was very fortunate to have found someone he truly loved and desired to be his companion in life; he had no doubt that after this mess was over, things would work out for them. Maybe someday he could count himself as one of the fortunate ones. He did not tell Bubba of his inclusion of Hattie and her family in the papers giving him his freedom; he wanted that bit of news to be a surprise. He thought it would make a perfect wedding gift.

Bill shifted in his chair and cleared his throat, bringing his and Bubba's attention back to the present, and the serious business at hand. He asked, "Bubba, how many men do you think would stay and be willing to fight? "The way I figure it, Bill, is that at least sixty percent of the able-bodied men will side with us. Some will be too afraid and some will simply leave the plantation and side with the Yankees." Bubba leaned back in his chair, and folded his arms across his chest, while saying, "What about you, Bill? Have you any idea how many white men and slaves from other plantations will join us?" "My best estimate is around two hundred men combined, and if these figures ring true that will give us a fighting force of approximately two hundred eighty men; more than enough to form a formidable militia. What about your parents, Bubba, how did they react when you told them?" "I know mama would stand as solid as a rock with me through thick and thin. You know how daddy likes to make jokes and he was true to form last night, but I could tell that deep down inside he is afraid; not afraid to fight if it comes to it, but afraid of the outcome this war will bring about, no matter who wins. I imagine this to be the attitude of most of the older people; they are treated well here and have settled into this way of life, and anything that interferes with the normal flow of things unnerves them. However, I feel once we explain and make them understand exactly what's going on and why they need to prepare for change, they will give us the emotional support we need in order to have a stable militia. I don't expect any of them to pick up a rifle if it comes to a fight, but it sure would be a sight to see."

Bubba, smiling broadly, continued, "I have to tell you Bill, mama and daddy both thought I had lost my mind when I first started talking; can't say as I much blame them with me just springing it on them like that. I could see the pride in mama's eyes when I finished talking and I could also tell that they had gained a new respect for you. I realize that you have put yourself at risk for all these years because of your determination to educate me. Since we're baring our souls this morning, I now want to say thank you, not only for my education but for being my friend, respecting me as a person, and for placing the trust in me that I know you would place in no other." "Bubba, both of us know mere words cannot describe this uncommon bond we have between us, but we do know it's the blind faith we have in each other, that holds us together. I want you to know that I am truly grateful for your trust in me as your Master, but most of all, as your friend." Bill held his hand out to Bubba, which Bubba took, clasping it tightly, and with a hoarseness in his voice, Bill said, "Well, Bubba, I suppose we'd better get down to business."

They sat there for a time discussing their plans, each in turn nervously watching out the window for the first sign of daylight, at which time they would sound the bell on the front porch. Whenever those living on the plantation heard this signal, they all knew to gather in front of the Big House to hear news that Bill wanted to share with them; most times it was changes in their daily work routines and schedules. Today, they would be in for quite a shock!

Both Bill and Bubba could feel the nervousness in the pit of their stomachs as they saw daylight break through the window. The hour, the minute and the dreaded second had come; they both knew that once they walked through that door and uttered the words that would inspire some of these men to fight and possibly die for this land, there would be no turning back. Bill slowly stood up and said, "Well, Bubba, the time has come for us to take our place in history." Together they walked out the door, clasped the rope attached to the bell, and rang it three times.

CHAPTER SIX

As Bill and Bubba stood on the porch, people began appearing out of nowhere, coming from all different directions, gathering in front of the big house, anxiously awaiting the news that would guide their daily lives. Bill stepped forward, reminding himself to speak slowly so that they would have no trouble understanding him.

"I know that some of you have heard the rumors going around the plantations that say the Northerners want the South to set you slaves free; I tell you now that those rumors are true. The Southern states have refused to do this, and as of yesterday morning we left the Union and formed our own country, which will be called the Confederate States of America. The North regarded this action taken by us as an Act of War, so the South felt that they had no choice but to fire on Ft. Sumter. This response has marked the beginning of a civil war. The Yankees say they will fight for your right to be free, and I have no doubt that they are marching south even as I speak, with every intention of doing so. To the South, this war is not about slavery but our right to govern our lives as we see fit. It should be left to us to work out our problems, and when I say us, I mean slaves and whites alike. You all know that even in your daily lives it takes time to solve big problems. Time is the healer of all wounds, and slavery is about as big a wound as a country can get. The Yankees don't want to give us time because they can't wait to get their greedy hands on the riches the South has to offer. They will rape this land for all it's worth, leaving you with barely a pot to piss in, and you can forget about having a window to throw it out of." Bill stopped to clear his throat, his mouth felt really dry. He was thinking, "I should have thought to keep some water handy." However, Bill continued, saying, "Forgive me for speaking so plainly, but I feel strongly that the freedom the Yankees want to offer you would leave you with a bitter taste in your mouths for years to come. As soon as they get what they want, they will quickly forget about you and all the promises I am quite sure they will make to you.

I speak to you today not as slaves, but as men who will soon have to make a choice in deciding which road you want to take. The road filled with empty promises or the road filled with the hope that one day you will be able to live and work in this land that you love, as free men. Without you there would be no glorious South. It is only because of you that we have prospered; the fields are soaked with your sweat and blood. You have already paid a dear price to call this land home. The Yankees promise you freedom, freedom to wander throughout the country homeless, with no means of feeding your families and relying on their charity just to survive from day to day."

Bill looked at Bubba as if seeking approval of his words thus far. Bubba winked at him, giving him the confidence to continue. "I dare not stand before you and try to tell you that slavery is right; it's about as wrong as you can get. If I had my way you would be working as free men, drawing fair wages for your labor and not forced to do the bidding of any man. Believe me when I say that I am not alone in my thinking; there are plenty of white men who feel as I do. Voicing our opinion on slavery in the past would have caused us to be branded as traitors; voicing our opinion at this time would cause us to be shot as traitors and any hope of a true freedom for you would die with us. We believe that there are many slaves throughout the South who would be willing to join forces with whites and fight the Yankees and throw them out of our homeland. This act of loyalty on the part of slaves would lay heavy on the hearts of white southerners. When the South wins this war, we will step forward and push for new laws that would in time ban slavery; the time will be right for reform. For those of you, and I know there are many who consider this land your home, the time is fast approaching when you will have to leave it or stay and fight for it. This is the only home that you, your parents and grandparents have ever known. This is the land where your children were and will be born and will one day be able to walk free with their heads held high. I know that some of you don't agree with the things I've said, but I'm asking you to hear me out. I can only say to those of you who choose to fight with us that freedom comes with a price for any man, black or white, and it's only those who are willing to pay that price who will achieve true freedom. There is hope for a future for you in the South, not as slaves, but as men who will have earned the right to be called true southerners; taking part in all the freedoms that the South has to offer anyone."

Bill noticed the lack of response he was getting from the slaves; there was only what seemed to be stunned silence. It was as if they had gone into some form of shock. This observation did not deter him. "I have always been honest and fair with you and I now ask that we band together to protect our land, our families, and a way of life that we cherish. The plantation owners and town officials have agreed to form a militia. I know this will be hard for you to believe, but it will be made up of black and white soldiers whose duty it will be to defend the town and protect the surrounding plantations. It will be formed with volunteers only, from both races. I will be its commanding officer with the rank of Captain; all officers in the unit at the insistence of the town officials, will be white. Seeing that none of us have any military experience, the officers among them that do will have to train us in the art of war. I figure that we have about two months to prepare ourselves; it will take the Yankees that long to find out where Folsom is." Bill's attempt at humor was not lost on the slaves, as this brought a chuckle from most of them. He thought, that's good, at least now I know that they're actually listening to me. "The weapons and uniforms we will need should be arriving any day, now that war has been declared. Hell, if the Yankees do attack us and see black men in Confederate uniforms pointing rifles at them, they'll most likely drop dead from shock." Laughter erupted from the slaves and he had to wait until it subsided before he could continue.

"You will be trained in the proper use of all weapons given to us, mainly the rifle and bayonet. We will not be confronting the enemy head on. We will strike the enemy only when we have the advantage in doing so without taking too many casualties. Our job is to hold the Yankees by keeping them confused until a larger force can arrive; we are to be kept informed as to the whereabouts of that force at all times. For those of you who will choose to join us, your training will begin one week from today. That will give you enough time to think about the things I've said very carefully and talk it over with your family and friends. This is the most important decision you'll most likely have to make in your entire lives. When the Yankee soldiers come, and believe me they will come, those of you who decide not to join us will be free to leave the plantation and take your chances on their promises. And I will bid you go with Godspeed. I cannot blame a man for doing what in his heart he feels is the right thing. I told you earlier that the plantation owners and town officials wanted no black man to hold a rank above private, but I will convince them to make an exception to that rule. I have chosen Bubba to be my aide. He will hold the rank of Lieutenant in charge of black troops and will answer only to me." It took all Bill could do not to laugh when he saw the expression on Bubba's face. It was one of those, what in the hell have you gotten me into now, looks.

"You all know Bubba as my manservant, but the time for truth has come. He is my friend and a man that I would trust with my very life. I also know that you respect and trust his judgment and have looked up to him as a leader. I have asked him to speak to you about this Civil War and tell you how he feels it will affect your lives." Bubba was thinking, Bill's father thought he would make a good lawyer someday, but I would put my money on Baptist preacher.

As Bubba stepped forward Bill gave him a look of encouragement, which Bubba desperately needed at this moment. He had spoken at the church meetings from time to time, but never before such a crowd as this. He took a deep breath, cleared his throat and began to speak.

"Well, I guess we're really in a fine mess. Last night we went to bed as slaves and we woke this morning with all the white folks promising us freedom. The North says they want to free us now, the South says they will give us freedom in their own time; when they are prepared to do so and will not be told what to do or when to do it by the North. The truth is, we as a people are not prepared for instant freedom without it having any foundation to it." Bubba could feel the sweat pouring from his body as he nervously spoke. "Most of us can't read or write and know nothing about the skills needed to survive in a white man's world. This instant freedom that the North wants to thrust upon us with no plan for our survival as a people, will spell disaster. It would be like sending your children into the fields to tend crops without first teaching them how, and we all know that would turn into a mess.

I believe that our only salvation is in taking it upon ourselves to prepare for this freedom and not fall victim to promises of assistance that will be made by the Yankees, and which I, too, have no doubt will be broken. If we should start out relying on the Yankees for handouts it will become a way of life for us. We've worked hard all our lives for white people and made them rich; just think about what we could do in this world if we put that same effort into helping ourselves."

Bubba noticed his fellow slaves looking at him as if he were a stranger and whispering among themselves. He spotted Hattie's brother, Sammy, in the crowd and asked him what the trouble was. "Bubba, you talkin and soundin like a white man, what done happen to you?" Bubba had become so passionate about what he wanted to say to the people gathered before him that he was totally unaware of the fact that he was not using the broken form of English spoken by slaves.

Bill, realizing the situation Bubba was in, quickly came to his aid. He walked over to him and said, "I am releasing you from your promise, it's alright to tell them the truth, because at this stage of the game I'm sure the South has more things to worry about than one slave being able to read and write. I don't want you to go through this ordeal we're about to enter with the added burden of keeping a secret of this magnitude."

Bubba gazed at the crowd before him, his eyes coming to rest on Sammy and said, "What happened to me is exactly what I wish will someday happen to all of you. Master Bill put himself in harms way by teaching me how to read and write when I was a mere boy." Sammy shouted, "You mean to say that you been makin fools out of us and laughin bout it since you was a boy?" Before Bubba could answer, his mother pushed her way to the front of the crowd and demanded to be heard. "Ya'll, listen to me! His daddy and me just found out bout it last night and I know ya'll don't think he been tryin to make fools out of us; ya'll know in your hearts that Bubba wouldn't do a thang like that. There is a good reason for him not tellin us, so I'm askin ya'll to please give him a chance to talk." She turned to Bubba and said, "Gone and tell them son, these folks is just like family, they'll understand." Bubba, encouraged by his mother's spirited support, began.

"As Master Bill already told you, over the years we have become best friends and there is an unspoken bond between us that no one can break. I know it's a strange thing, but it was just like it was meant to be from the day we first met as boys. He's taught me many things that we all need to know in order to survive in the world away from this plantation. I've most likely read every book in his library and everything else I could get my hands on. Yes, this man has educated me knowing that if we were caught it would mean trouble for both of us; they'd more than likely hang me, they'd probably just stop speaking to him." Sammy was the first one to start laughing and said, "Boy, you may talk like a white man but you still crazy as evah." "That's exactly it, Sammy. I'm still the same Bubba who loves his people and would do anything to protect ya'll, and my way of protecting you was by not telling you. If word had gotten out that there was an educated slave on this plantation, there would have been hell to pay for everyone. All I could do was wait for the time to come when I would be able to use this knowledge to help my people; that time has finally come. Mama is right, we're all family, and even as a boy I dreamed of sharing my knowledge with all of my family. Master Bill once told me when we were just boys, that he was going to educate me so he'd have someone to talk with about worldly things. I want my family to become educated so they'll have the tools to survive in this newfound freedom that one way or another is sure coming. This will be my first order of business during and after this Civil War; my parents will be my first two students, and guess who's going to be the third, casting his gaze at Sammy. I'm going to teach him so good that even white folks will think he's a white man who has spent a little too much time in the sun." Laughter filled the air, with shouts of approval. Bubba silently thanked God for his mama; she had saved him from what could have turned into a bad situation. He continued, "It is my choice to side with Master Bill on this matter. Not because he's my friend, but because I believe it is the best course of action for us to take. Which one of you would ever have dreamed, let alone thought, that a slave would ever be allowed to stand before you and speak freely on the things I have talked about?" Old man Victor, who was standing in the middle of the crowd, was the first to speak. "I nevah thought I'd live to see this day; just standin here talkin bout thangs right out in the open, we been haven to hide in our cabins to talk bout, is kinda scary. I'm an old man and I seen black folks lynched for sayin and doin a whole lot less than you have today. If this is what freedom taste like, I show likes it! I'm with you, son." Bubba knew that Victor's endorsement would go a long way in helping the others make their decision. Miss Addie, the woman that Sammy was soon to marry, spoke up. "This plantation is my home and I ain't goin nowhere, but I don't want to fight anyone either. God meant for us to live in peace and learn to love one another; I know sometimes it's a hard thang to do but we have to try and do what He says." Bubba replied, "It would be a true blessing if all men would do that, but the devil is hard at work rounding up evil men to do his bidding in this world, and from the looks of things he'll have no short supply. However, I do understand and respect your feelings about this and would not dare think of asking you to leave your home. Those of you who choose to remain here, but not fight the Yankees, will be allowed to do so. If it comes down to it, people will be needed to tend to the sick and wounded and perform other duties that would bring comfort to our soldiers." A voice was demanding to be heard from the back of the crowd; Bubba looked on as Miss Martha (Hattie's mama), shoved her way forward. His stomach started doing flips; he sure didn't place himself on the list of one of her favorite people. To his surprise, when Martha finally reached the front she turned her attention not to him, but to Bill. Martha placed her hands on her rather large hips, and began to speak. "Master Bill, you could not have picked a finer man to be your friend than Bubba. I been watchin him ovah the years, always goin out of his way to help other folks and not lookin for nothin in return. He has a good heart and any mother would be proud to call him her son. I knew your granddaddy and he was a mean man, treated us like we was some kind of animals stead of like human beins. When he passed on, there show wasn't no moanin and cryin bout it. We praised God that Master James, your daddy, he still treated us as slaves put here only to do his biddin, but he was a fair man, and didn't try to work us into the ground. I remember the day he married and brought your mama here. The very next mornin she was out and bout the plantation; Lord it was a hot day for pickin cotton. The sweat was just pourin off me. I felt somebody standin next to me so I turned to see who it was, and there stood your mama with a pail of water offerin me a drink and askin me if I was feelin all right. I never had a white person to ax me how I was feelin or even care. I came down bad off sick a few weeks aftah that; it was like all my strength had gone. If it hadn't been for her I would not have been long for this world. That woman would show up at my cabin evahday to help my family nurse me back to good health. I found out later that she was also helpin other slaves when they was sick or just plain wore out. Long as I live I won't nevah forgit your mama and I prays for her soul evah night. Bubba don't have to tell most of us what a good man you are; I seen your mama in you a long time ago. There ain't nobody standin here that can say a cross word bout you; cause you been kind to us and have treated us like family stead of slaves. Us bein slaves ain't a fault of yo's; we was in this mess long befoe you was born, you just sort of got stuck with it. The thangs that you done for Bubba tells me that your mama is still livin on through you, and I know that she would nevah have done anythin that would brang harm to us. You might not make the white folks in the South see the need for us to be free, but I knows in my heart that ya'll tries your best to make it be."

65

Bill was quite moved by Martha's words and hoped his mother, looking down from heaven, heard the profound difference she had made in the lives of most of these people. He silently prayed that her spirit would guide him to do the same. Several men had gathered behind Martha as she spoke. When she finished having her say, one of them shouted, "We all agree that Master Bill is a good man and will do as he says. What bout those of us that don't want to wait til the Yankees come, and want to leave the plantation now?" Several of the men in the crowd cheered him on. "Wees take our chances on makin it to the North, where freedom is just waitin for us." Bubba knew the man who was speaking; his name was Meatball. He didn't know how he came by such a name, but it seemed to fit him. He got drunk at every opportunity and attempted to stir up trouble on the plantation, most of it directed at other slaves. Bubba remembered that he had to put him in his place a time or two for trying to bully the weakest men among them. If there were ever a list drawn up naming fools among men, Meatball's name would surely be on it. Meatball was a bull of a man; he stood well over six feet tall, and his skin was as black as a moonless night. Meatball's huge bald head glistened in the sunlight, his face, and cold, dark eyes had a menacing look about them, sending a warning, "You don't wanna mess with me!" as clear as a bell. This was exactly the type of man that would be turned down if he applied to join the militia; there would be no controlling this type of individual, black or white. Bubba decided that it would be better to deal with this situation now, rather than later. "Master Bill and I have no desire to keep any one of you who choose not to join us from seeking your freedom. The things that have been shared with you today were shared out of respect for you as individuals, in the hope that when the time comes you will have enough information to make the choice you feel is right for you and your family. You and I know that there most likely is not a slave in the whole state of South Carolina that's enjoying the freedom to speak out without fear, as we are doing today. Master Bill has put his trust in you that the things said here today, which we all know go against southern law, will remain here. Trust goes both ways." Bubba had managed to overcome his nervousness, and was now speaking with new confidence. "Master Bill has taken a big chance on you today. He and all of us stand to lose a great deal if what has gone on here were ever found out. Although the other plantations have agreed to form a militia including both races, they would rise up against Master Bill if they knew of his other plans for us, and sooner or later, all slaves throughout the South. Have no doubt that I, and those who agree with me, will have no pity on any man who dishonors that trust. We cannot allow anyone to leave here before the Yankees are in sight of our guns. Then, and only then, will you be allowed to leave this plantation and try to make it to the North. We simply cannot take the chance of the Yankees finding out our plans for defending the town and plantations in case of an attack."

Bubba paused, staring at the crowd for a long moment before his voice rang out, strong and clear. "As a slave, this is a very hard thing for me to say, but it needs saying straight out. If anyone takes it in his or her head to sneak off this plantation before the time we've set, I personally will chase you down and bring you back, and it will be left up to you how you come back; I think everyone gets my meaning. The secrecy of our plan must be protected at any cost." Bill, seeing how much Bubba was affected by having to say those words, stepped forward saying, "I know this has been a day like no other you've ever had in your lives. You have a lot to think about and rightly so; therefore no work will be required of you today. Use this time to think and talk about what was said here, and may God guide you in making your choice. I will be leaving this afternoon for Folsom to meet with the other plantation owners. We will discuss other defense plans, receive our military commissions and be given the supplies we will need to carry out our duties. In my absence, Bubba will be in charge of the plantation and will be making a list of everyone who decides to join the militia, and answering any questions you may have. I thank those that put their trust in me and will speak to you again when I return."

Bubba smiled at the crowd standing before him and spoke to them once more, "Master Bill not only has given us the day off, he is also providing food and drink for everyone. Return to your cabins and put on your Sunday best, cause we gone have us a down home picnic. You boys know that I'm partial to a little home brew now and then, mostly now stead of then; so if it's all gone by the time I get to the barn this afternoon, this mama's boy gone be mighty upset." The sound of laughter came from the crowd as they started back to their cabins to prepare for the picnic.

CHAPTER SEVEN

Bill and Bubba returned to the study. Bill walked straight to the cabinet where he kept his liquor, grabbed a bottle of brandy and two glasses. "It's a bit early in the morning, Bubba, but I think we've earned this drink today." "I couldn't agree with you more, my friend. When I saw Miss Martha pushing her way toward me in that crowd, I could have used this drink to stop my knees from shaking. You have no idea how relieved I was when she started talking to you." Bill laughed. "Bubba, are you really that afraid of her?" "Afraid is a strong word, Bill, let's just say I know that my upsetting her would not be good for my health." "From what you've told me of her, I can see your point." They smiled at each other as they thought of her favorite weapon.

"Bubba, I must admit that she was right about my grandfather and father. I was quite moved when she spoke of the kindness and caring my mother showed the slaves." Bill felt the pain of his mother's absence, as he said, "It seems that both our mothers saved the day for us."

"I wish you could have seen the look on your face when I said that you are going to be my aide, in charge of all black troops." "Yeah, you really got me with that one, but I'm not sure if that's really a good idea." Bubba stood up, and began pacing the floor, as he talked. "Bill, the white soldiers and officers will resent it; a black man with some authority is probably their worst nightmare." "Don't worry about it, Bubba, I'll smooth it over somehow. The black soldiers will need someone of their own race to look up to; you're qualified and you're it. You'll only have command of the black troops; that should not ruffle their white feathers too much. And don't forget, this militia will be made up of volunteers only; they will know up front what they are getting themselves into. Those who oppose a black officer being in the ranks won't sign up anyway." "Bill, you're a sneaky rascal. You've had this figured out all along haven't you?" With a sheepish grin, Bill replied, "I guess you could say that." "Well, I certainly hope you don't have any more surprises in store for me," Bubba laughed as he made a fist and pointed it towards Bill's head. Bill poured two large drinks and handed Bubba a glass. "It has been a very stressful morning, my friend, for both of us."

They found it to be relaxing just to talk about the lighter moments of the meeting and drink brandy for a while; serious matters could wait a few hours. "Now, tell me how that man came to be named Meatball?" Bill asked. "I swear, Bill, as many times as I've told you how we give people their nicknames, you never seem to catch on. This is the last time I am going to explain it to you, so please pay attention. Most of us get our nicknames when we are young; it could come from our physical appearance, the constant craving of some type of food, or some idiotic thing we were caught doing." "Alright Bubba, I think that I have finally caught on; let's see if I've got this right. Do you remember when we were boys how we use to raid the kitchen, and the cook almost caught you stealing hot fried chicken off the stove, and you were only saved from being found out because you shoved the hot chicken leg down your pants? Lucky for you your back was turned toward her." "Yes, Bill, I remember that too well; I had blisters on my pecker for a week." "So, from what you said about how nicknames are given, it would be alright for me to call you chicken pecker?" Bubba squinted his eyes at Bill and said, "It's gonna be a sad day when my mama sees me hanging from a tree." "What makes you say a thing like that, Bubba?" "Because I'm getting ready to kill me a white man; you caught on too good." "Well, my friend, let's just chalk it up to your being a good teacher. However, if you think I am ever going

72

to forget that crowning moment in your life, you are sadly mistaken." Bubba retorted by replying, "Alright, have it your way, Master snake ass." "Bubba, that's not playing fair and you know it." "Who's concerned about fair? If that snake had bitten you, there would have been three holes in your ass." "Bubba, I guess you realize you're putting our friendship on shaky ground with that remark." "Well, the ground is about to split wide open because I remember the time...." and on they went, back and forth, having the time of their lives, recalling humorous moments in their youth and tricks they'd played on one another over the years. It was as though both men were trying to hold on to the things that made their friendship solid in order to fortify themselves against the horror they knew was coming soon.

Wiping his eyes from laughing so hard, Bill finally managed, "Well, Bubba, it's time to get down to some serious business; my showing up drunk at the meeting in Folsom would not exactly instill confidence in my ability to command. How many men have you trained in the use of the rifle on those hunting trips?" Bubba, rubbing his chin, replied, "I've got ten men that I would consider fair shots and three that shoot like they were born to it. I picked these men to train because I know they can be trusted to follow orders to the letter and if they decide to join us, they certainly would stand out as examples to the others; plus help to keep order and the morale up among the men if the going gets rough." "That type of thinking is exactly why I picked you for my aide; you thought through every detail before you made your decision and that shows the ability you have to lead." "I can't help but wonder, Bill, if I'll maintain that ability when someone starts shooting at me. Making decisions when bullets aren't flying is totally different from making them when they are, especially if they are flying in your direction." "The truth, Bubba, is that you and I, whether you want to admit it or not, are cursed or blessed, however you see it, with putting the well-being of others before our own needs. We have lived our lives this way and it will ring true even in battle; we are who we are and nothing can change that. Think about what Miss Martha said about us this morning. People like her have the gift to see deep into a person's soul, and thank God she saw a lot of goodness in ours. So put those negative thoughts out of your mind, Bubba. When the time comes, we both will do what's right to protect those trusting us with their lives."

"Now, back to the business at hand. Needless to say, the normal functions of this plantation will have to be changed to meet our needs. We will need to clear some land, enough to accommodate the training camp. The Army will supply us with tents and cots for housing the men and anything else we will need to establish the camp. Naturally, we'll have to increase our food supply. Also our soldiers will simply have to be made to understand that we cannot allow their personal lives to interfere with their military training." "I agree with you on that Bill. It probably would be wise to put the camp as far away from the rest of the population as possible. I know of a spot that's about five miles from here that would be perfect."

"Good thinking, Bubba," Bill said, admiration in his voice. "You'll also have to take charge of things until my return. Then, we can coordinate our efforts and rush to complete the things that will still need to be done. I'll be relying on you to make the necessary work schedule and assign the men wherever you feel they are needed in order to accomplish the tasks ahead of us. I'm sure glad that I trusted my instincts and never hired an overseer to run this plantation. Most of them are cruel men, and I have no doubt that he would have been challenging your authority every step of the way. If you have to pull men from the fields to lend you a hand, do it. My grandfather and father had their faults, but thank God they knew how to make sound investments. I'll be fine, financially, if I never grow another crop. If necessary, I'll hire some men with wagons to help bring back the supplies from Folsom. I know how you worry about everything, so if it takes more time than I've figured on, I'll send a rider to let you know. I guess I'd better start preparing for my trip.

The morning is wasting away and I must be on my way by noon. Take care, my friend, I leave everything in your capable hands." Bubba nodded and said, "I'll get the men started on clearing the ground in the morning; at least those who aren't sick from too much celebrating today. I know that most of them are waiting for me at the barn, full of home brew and questions. Have a safe trip, Bill, and don't forget to look in on your lady friend; I think you've earned a bit of relaxation." As Bubba got up to leave, Bill just smiled at him and shook his head.

As Bill packed his bags, he wondered what the state of affairs would be in Folsom; one of crisis, or just a calm resolve to do what one must to protect their homes. The attitude of most (he recalled from the last meeting), showed him their almost complete ignorance concerning war. They had the audacity to think this war with the Yankees would be like a turkey shoot. They believed that they could dress up in their fancy uniforms, mount their pretty horses (with bands playing), draw their shiny new sabers, and run the Yankees out of the South in a matter of weeks. Bill knew that this would definitely not be the case, but he hesitated in educating them on the realities of war; not because he did not want to dampen their spirit, but it simply would have been unwise to give them his honest view at this particular time. The last thing he needed was to be branded as a Yankee sympathizer. He would just have to wait and see when he arrived if any attitudes had changed now that war had actually been declared. However, he decided his first order of business would be to take heed of Bubba's advice and seek out his lady friend. He decided that relaxing with her for a few hours probably would help to relieve the stress he'd been under these past few days, and as was his habit, he smiled to himself.

CHAPTER EIGHT

Bubba started walking toward the barn, the favorite gathering place for the men, when not working; they told tall tales, drank homemade brew, and discussed anything that came to mind. He had no doubt as to what the topic of conversation would be today. His intention was to pass by his cabin, but he noticed a group of people sitting on his porch; he heard his daddy's voice raised above all the others. He decided to stop and see what the commotion was all about. When Louie looked up and saw him approaching, he said, "Here comes Bubba now, you ax him for yo'self." Bubba, with a puzzled look on his face, demanded to know exactly what was going on. His daddy turned to old man Barrow and said, "Go ahead and ax him, the Lord is walkin with this boy, he ain't gone refuse you." Bubba glanced at the people sitting on the porch. He noticed that every one of them were the elderly members belonging to the Sunday morning prayer group. Old man Barrow was the most senior member, so he was the one that led them in prayer and song every Sunday, rain or shine. Bubba looked at him and was a bit shocked by what he saw. Mr. Barrow's hands were shaking, as he held up what seemed to be a Bible. "Where in the world did you get that, Mr. Barrow? Is that a Bible?" "It show is, son; I've kept this Good Book hidden for years. A white preacher who was run out of Folsom for preachin gainst slavery, give it to me. When I was a young man, Mr. Bill's daddy would send me to pick up supplies in town once a week. On that particlar day I saw this buggy pulled longside the road; my mind told me that somethin was wrong, just didn't look right that buggy just sittin there like that. I go over to it and sees this white man laid out on the seat, blood was all over his face, look like somebody done beat him somethin awful. He could hardly talk; his eyes look like they was pleadin with me to help him. I didn't want to get mixed up in white folk's business, but I just couldn't find it in me to walk away and leave like him that. It was like the Lord was testin me just to see if I was truly a chile of His. I took him to a cabin bout a mile from that road; nobody had lived there for years, so I figure he be safe there and have nough time to mend. I cleaned him up best as I could, gave him some water and left him part of the meal I always took with me on them trips. It was easy for me to sneak over there evahday and do what I could to help him get his strength back. I done that for bout two weeks. Come the day he was able to leave, he thanked me for the kindness I showed him and gave me this Bible. He said, "I know you can't read and that it's gainst the law for you to have this book, so you keep it well hid. When troubled times come into yo life you just grab hold of this Good Book and you'll feel the power and the love of the Lord flowin through you. It will give you the strength to endure any hardship that's put upon you."

That preacher said, "One day a man would come that holds the keys to the chains of slavery that bind you. You will know him by the words of hope he gives you and your people for a better life. Then and only then will you take this book from its hidin place and give it to him. He will read wondrous stories that tell of God's love for all people and of the reward that awaits those who have put their everlastin faith in him." Mr. Barrow held the Bible out to Bubba. "Take it, son. When I heard you talkin this mornin, the words that preacher said long ago come back to me jus like it was yestiday and I knew right then that you was the one he spoke of. Befoe that white preacher went on his way, he made me promise to do xactly as he said. So, Bubba, please take this Good Book and read the words to us that will someday set our souls free."

Bubba was so touched and so surprised by this man's words that he was almost speechless. He thought, what in the world have I gotten myself into? I only want to help them, not be looked upon as some kind of savior. But he knew he dare not insult this man by refusing to do what he had asked of him. What harm could it do anyway? After all, he was a Christian and believed in God with all his heart, and if reading the Bible to them would help to reinforce their faith, then so be it.

Bubba took the book, opened it, and began to read. It had been quite a while since he had actually read the Bible, and after reading for awhile even he became caught up in the overpowering feelings of hope. Just like the old man said, he felt the power of the Lord rushing through his body as the words seemed to take hold of him and sanction the path he had chosen to help his people. As he finished reading the last verse of the 23rd Psalm, he closed the book. The look on the faces before him said more than any words could ever say; it was a look of total contentment. He attempted to give the Bible back to Mr. Barrow, but the old man refused It. "You keep it, son, I have kept my promise to that preacher; it is now left to you to grab hold of it when you need to find the strength to carry on." All of the Elders thanked him and began leaving. Then, as if on cue, they starting singing a spiritual that he had not heard since he was a boy; Lord won't you lead me and guide me along the way.

Louie walked over to his son and put his arms around him giving him a big hug. "Bubba, your mama and me be so proud of you that we can't even find the words to tell you how much. I guess you know by now that most of the older people are with you; the younger folks I'm not so sure bout, they ain't too long on patience." "Thank you, daddy, I knew you'd come around to my way of thinking. After all, I'm only living my life the way that you taught me. Where is mama? I figured she'd be here relaxing and enjoying this free time with you." "Yo mama and the other ladies done gone to cookin for the picnic, they ain't got no time for us men folk right now; so we just let them do the cookin and wees do the eatin!" "Well, daddy, I think I'll head over to the barn and find out which way the tide is turning with the younger folks; it's gonna take some tall convincing with some of them because as you said, being long on patience is not a virtue of most of the young."

He noticed as he approached the barn, that men were gathered outside and had formed a circle; he instinctively knew there was a fistfight going on. Sure enough, when he finally reached and forced his way through the circle of men, there was Edmond (Hattie's older brother), on the ground bleeding badly from the nose and mouth. Meatball was standing over him gesturing and saying, "Come on, get up, so I can knock you down again! You want to take up for Bubba, you gone pay the price! He ain't evah proved hisself to be a man, and all that readin and writin don't make him one. I'm the best man round here and he gone have to beat me with his fists, not them fancy words. If he wants to be a leader, he gone have to show us that he can lead when the fightin starts."

Bubba had known it would come to this someday. In the past, he was always able to talk Meatball into submission. However, today would be a different story. There was no getting around the fact that he had to fight Meatball and win decisively. This was the unwritten law among men who only knew how to prove themselves as men by testing their physical strength against each other.

Bubba silently thanked God for Bill, who while in his travels to the North and Europe, was introduced to and became very good at the art of boxing. He remembered spending quite some time being Bill's punching bag until he finally caught on. That was the day he unintentionally knocked Bill senseless. His eyes rolled back in his head, he fell to the floor so hard Bubba thought surely someone heard him; it almost scared Bubba to death. When Bill came back to his senses, he looked up at Bubba and said, "Guess I'm a pretty good teacher, huh?" From that day on they would spar several days a week without doing bodily harm to one another. He finally became Bill's equal at boxing and often wondered how he would do in a real fight. He was about to find out if his years of training would pay off; no doubt his days of wondering would soon be over.

Bubba also knew that he had to find a way to make a friend of this man instead of a sworn enemy. The men that looked up to Meatball would easily follow if he could be persuaded to join the militia. However, first he had to win the fight and somehow leave him with his dignity.

Meatball spotted Bubba as he came through the crowd of men. He was walking over to Edmond, with the intention of helping him to his feet. Meatball shouted, "You best leave him down there cause you gone be joinin him in a few minutes!" "Can't we talk about this, Meatball? There is no call for us to fight each other. This is a time for us to come together and work for the good of all. We can't have unity if we're busy fighting among ourselves." "Talkin won't save you this time Bubba, and Master Bill ain't here to save you from this butt whippin either; next time he see you he ain't gone recognize his lackey." With that remark, Meatball walked up to Bubba with a determined look in his eyes and without hesitation connected his fist with Bubba's head, which sent him staggering backward for several feet. Bubba became slightly dazed from the blow but recovered quickly. Meatball charged at him as if he were a bull; Bubba sidestepped him, while at the same time sending a blow to his stomach, which seemed to knock the breath out of him. "Let's end this now, Meatball, this proves nothing." In between breaths Meatball replied, "Oh no! Mr. Lackey, you ain't gettin off that easy," as he took a swing at Bubba's head. Bubba managed to duck that blow and several more that were sent his way; he began to feel his training starting to take hold and that gave him the confidence he needed to win this fight. Meatball charged once more. This time Bubba caught him with an uppercut, knocking him to the ground. He somehow managed to get on his feet. Just as Bubba came toward him, he threw a wild punch, which landed squarely on Bubba's chin. The force of the blow buckled his knees. Both men were slightly dazed and tired. Bubba stood up slowly as Meatball watched; he did not want to make the mistake of charging Bubba again. Suddenly, with arms raised and in motion, Bubba began to circle him coming in closer with each circle he made. When he was close enough, he sent two jabs to his head and sort of danced backward out of harm's way. Bubba kept jabbing at Meatball's head until his face became a bloody mess. It wasn't that Meatball wasn't trying to return the punches; the problem was that Bubba moved so swiftly, Meatball couldn't land any punches. Finally, completely frustrated, he mumbled through his swollen lips,   "Why don't you stan still and fight like a man? I ain't nevah seen nobody fight like you." "That's why I want to educate you Meatball," said Bubba. "Think of this as your first lesson." Meatball became so angry with Bubba that he lost control and made the mistake of charging at him head on, running right into a fist that knocked him out cold.

Bubba had noticed the strange behavior of the men watching the fight. With most fights, men were yelling and screaming for their favorite to beat the hell out of his opponent. Throughout, and even after this fight, there was only silence. It was as if they realized that the outcome of this fight would decide their future. Bubba yelled, "Somebody bring me some water." His brother, David, came over and handed him a pail, which Bubba threw on Meatball's face. Confused, Meatball shook himself and looked up at Bubba saying, "Well, I guess you can go on and brag bout how you a better man than me; you beat me fair and square. How did you learn that fancy way of fightin?" "In the world away from this plantation there are quite a few things that are done differently, and we'll have to learn to do them in order to survive. All I want to do, Meatball, is to help prepare us for the time when freedom comes knocking at our door. We'll need strong men like you to help guide, lead and protect our people. The men and I still respect you because you stood up for what you believed to be right. I won the fight because I fought in a way that you don't know. If I had fought by your rules, you probably would have beaten the hell out of me. I only hope that now, at least you will give what Master Bill and I are trying to accomplish here, a chance. I need you to stand by my side and help me to lead these men, not only into battle, but also into their future."

The other men finally broke their silence. They gave a loud cheer, shouting approval of what Bubba had said. Bubba leaned down and helped Meatball to his feet and said, "What do you say?" The men grew quiet again. A smile broke out on Meatball's swollen face as he said, "I nevah thought I'd hear myself sayin this, Bubba, but I'll stand with you; I ain't crazy nough to let you get all the glory." Meatball held out his hand. Bubba took his hand and said, "I sure hope ya'll got some of that homebrew left in the barn cause me and Meatball show need some." The men were laughing and cheering their leaders as they followed them into the barn.

CHAPTER NINE

The time to celebrate the morning events was at hand. Bubba and Meatball sat down on a bale of hay and eagerly took the cups of homebrew handed to them, gulped them down and held their cups out for more. No one mentioned the fight, it seemed that everyone just wanted to have a good time and enjoy this day, which was fine with Bubba. As he glanced at the faces of the men gathered there, he felt honored to be among them and yet unworthy of the trust and faith they were now putting in him. He vowed to himself that he would remain humble and not let this go to his head, and always, try to act in their best interest. His brother Jab, who was already slightly drunk, walked over to him saying, "Pretty good brew, huh? You know I thank I'm gonna be the first one to sign up for the militia." Sammy yelled, "Yeah, you could kill at least ten Yankees with yo breath!" Jab yelled back, "Your sister didn't seem to mind last night!" Laughter filled the barn at this good-natured joking.

Bubba saw that the men were in rare form today, so he decided to go along and join them in their funny way of humiliating each other. He said, "Jab may get drunk but he ain't ever got drunk enough to go up against Miss Martha and her fryin pan. Ain't that right, Arthur? And, Arthur, you never did tell us how you got that knot on your head." "I'm tellin ya'll a mule kicked me in the head a week befoe I married Rosa," Arthur replied. Leo (one of Hattie's other brothers) shouted, "You callin my mama a mule?" "I ain't said nothin bout yo mama", Arthur insisted. "Oh," said Leo, "So what you mean to say was that my mama hit you in the head with that fryin pan so hard that it felt like a mule kicked you in the head." Even Arthur had to laugh at the way Leo put it. Suddenly David said, "Bubba, I don't know why you laughin so hard. You must of forgot bout the time Master Bill gave that big shindig and all the rich white folks come up from Folsom wearin all them fancy clothes." Bubba looked puzzled. "What you talking about?" "Now, Bubba, don't sit there and tell me you done forgot bout that time you almost gave that white lady a heart attack? Well, seein that you claimin you don't rememba, let me help you out. You see ya'll, they was needin extra help up at the Big house with cookin the food and servin it to the folks. Mama took Jab and me long to help out. When we walks into the kitchen there was Bubba dressed up like a

Thanksgivin turkey. He had on those tight pans and was wearin one of them long coats like Master Bill wears when he's spectin company. Man, he sure looked pretty! Bubba was gone be servin the folks sometin called shampain; one of them fancy wines white folks drink. Anyways, he shows me where the cases of shampain was, and said every time he took out a tray of glasses filled with it, he wanted me to have another one waitin for him by time he come back. He come back bout thirty minutes later, and just like he told me, I had a tray waitin for him. But stead of takin the tray, this fool axed me for a raw sweet potato; the biggest one I could find. He takes the potato, looks around to make sure no one is watchin him, then shoves it inside the front of his pants. I knew right then my brother done lost his mind, but he says to me, don't say a word bout this, I will explain it to you later. Then he picks up the tray and leaves. Next thang I know I hear a lady screamin. I goes runnin out there and sees this white woman laid out on the floor; she done fainted dead away, lookin as white as a sheet. Folks was gathered all round her tryin to bring her back to her senses. When she comes to herself, they axed what the trouble was. She said she had too much wine, got dizzy from it, and started seein thangs. She begged Master Bill's pardon and said she had to leave at once. Bubba, who was standin right over her still holdin the tray, said, "M'am, is there anythang I can do for you?" Man, you should have seen that look she gave Bubba when she said, "No! Not for me or any other respectable white woman." When Bubba come back to the kitchen, I axed him what the hell was goin on. That's when he tole me that while he servin the wine he overheard this lady talkin, tellin folks she was from up North and how she never seen a black man up close befoe. Then she started talkin bout the rumors she heard goin round sayin black men had really big organs; that mean big peckers ya'll. Anyways, that's when Bubba decide to play a joke on her and comes back to get the potato. He said when he went back she was sittin on the sofa by herself, so he walked up as close to her as he could without seemin disrespectful, and held the tray up high so she would have a good view of his private parts, sayin, "Would you like somethin M'am?" When that woman looked up, the first thang she saw was what she done thought was Bubba's pecker hangin halfway down his leg. Them tight pants he was wearin didn't leave no doubt in her mind. Lord have mercy! That woman started screamin like the house was on fire and fainted dead away. It took all Bubba could do to keep a straight face through the whole thang. If she evah runs into Bubba in town, I bet you couldn't catch her even if you was ridin a racehorse."

Bubba, laughing with the rest of the crowd, said, "Since you telling everything David, why don't you tell us what happened to them four bottles of wine that come up missin that night?" "Well," said David, "I couldn't tell you back then cause it mighta caused me to get my head beat in; ain't that right Meatball? Seein that wees all friends now, I'm gone tell you jus what happened. While you was out servin the folks, Meatball come to the back door and said for me to come outside for a minute. When I gits out there, I sees that he has Hattie's brother, Otto, with him. He tells me to git him some of them white folk's fancy wine; I told him that I couldn't do nothin like that cause if I got caught there would be hell to pay. He give me that mean look of his and said that if I didn't do it there was gonna be hell to pay right now. I wasn't crazy nough to say no to him twice. So I goes and gits two bottles and gives them to him and that little runt that was wit him and they goes on off." Meatball was looking at David with a sheepish grin on his face, and David said, "Don't be lookin at me like that, cause I'm gone tell it all. After the shindig was over, all the folks started headin back to town. We started cleanin up the mess that was left and by the time we finished it was real late; I headed straight for the cabin. Man, I was tired. As I was passin by the hog pen I hear this fuss goin on so I stopped to see what it was. There was Otto passed out drunk in the middle of a bunch of hogs, lookin like they was tryin to decide who was gone take the first bite outa him. So I had to drag and carry him to his cabin. I don't know why that boy gits drunk like that. He know that his wife, Margaret, who is three times his size, gone beat him into next week and send him packin every time he do. I didn't see Meatball, but the next mornin I heard some boys talkin bout how they had to pull him out the creek that night; said he was talkin all crazy sayin sometin bout he gone swim back to Africa."

The men were laughing hard at the end of this story, but Bubba yelled out, "Hold on, David, now let me get this straight; you said you gave Meatball two bottles of wine, right?" "Did I say two? Well, I meant to say...." But before David could continue Bubba said, "Like you said, brother, if you gone tell it, tell it all." "Well alright," David said, looking a bit sheepish, "so I took two bottles for myself; I figures since I was headin for trouble anyways, I might as well enjoy some of that fancy wine too. Now ya'll knows that I truly do love to take me a drink, but after seein what that wine did to Meatball and Otto, I got to thinkin that maybe this wine is for white folks only, cause they was drinkin plenty of it and ain't none of them was actin a fool. The Lord is my witness. It was the first time in my life I was scared to take a drink, so I hid it under my bed and it been there evah since, and that been nearly three years ago. If ya'll think I'm lyin, I go and git it for you right now. Meatball, maybe you and Otto want to finish off them other two bottles today?" Meatball's eyes found Otto's in the crowd of men and at the same time they both said, "Hell, no!" Laughter followed this outburst, along with many more humorous stories, until a young boy appeared in the doorway of the barn and shouted, "The women say if ya'll don't come on and git ready to eat they gone feed the food to the hogs." With that bit of news the men started heading slowly for the door.

But before they left, Bubba stood and held up his hand. "Wait for just a minute, men. We need to take a little while and talk about the chores for tomorrow; then we can go get cleaned up and start eatin that fine meal the women have prepared for us. I've picked out the place where we're going to build the camp that will house the militia and also serve as our training area. We'll all meet here at daybreak to form work teams and start clearing the land in the morning. All of you men will at sometime or another be helping us to get set up. You men who decide to join up with the militia will get your chance to do it when Master Bill returns. He and I will talk to each man before we let him sign on; we have to make sure that each one is deciding to join us for the right reasons. Drink all you want and have your fun today, because starting tomorrow we get down to serious business. Now, what do you say we go and join the women before they really do give our food to the hogs."

Bubba spotted Edmond as they were leaving and called him over, saying, "I just want to thank you for standing up for me like that. What made you do it?" "I really don't know, Bubba. Meatball was just runnin his mouth talkin bout thangs he don't know nothin bout, and I was tired of him tryin to bully evahbody. Next thang I knows, I done took a swing at him. Besides, I couldn't have him bad mouthin my future brother-in-law, now could I?" Bubba looked startled, as Edmond laughed and said, "I may not say a lot but I sure sees a lot; you and my sister, Hattie, are gonna make a fine pair." He shook Bubba's hand and left without another word.

Bubba hurried to his cabin in order to wash up and change clothes. When he got there, his brothers were coming out of the door still putting on their clothes, saying, "We ain't got no time to waste, Bubba. Man, we hungry!" Bubba went inside and discovered that his parents, too, had already left for the festivities. It felt good to have a little time to himself. He thought about how well the day's events had gone; so far, God had been truly with him. Deciding to take a few minutes to begin figuring out the work teams for the next day, he went to his hiding place and removed pen and paper.

Bubba decided to have two teams of men do the clearing, and one team to do the actual building of the camp. He would put Sammy in charge of the building team. All you had to do was draw a picture of what you wanted and Sammy sure could build it; beat all he'd ever seen. Arthur and David would be put in charge of the other teams. The men respected them for their ability to work hard and not complain, and there surely would be hard work ahead. He would make Meatball his foreman. This would feed his ego enough for him to help keep the men that looked up to him in line, and also serve to stop any tension between the men. He was well aware of the fact that the peace he and Meatball made today was fragile, and like all fragile things he had to handle it gently.

Bubba suddenly realized that what seemed like minutes had actually been an hour. He jumped up, put away his notations, and prepared to get ready for the picnic, knowing that everyone would be waiting for his arrival. As he was getting dressed he thought about Hattie. It would be nice if he could spend some time alone with her. However, he knew that just to be near her would mean socializing with her brothers. He should tell Hattie exactly how he felt about her, because they would be seeing very little of each other due to the preparations for war. He wanted her to know that come hell or high water, he intended to marry her someday. With that thought in mind, he left the cabin and headed for the picnic with a spring in his step that only love can bring.

The ladies had lined tables up by the creek, the favorite place of everyone for picnics. He spotted his parents sitting at one of the tables and could not believe his luck; seated next to his parents were Hattie's folks, and this meant that he could be near her without drawing undue attention. Man, he thought, this is really gonna be a good day! His father was the first to see him coming toward them and said, "Bout time you decided to join us Bubba, for awhile there I was thinkin maybe you went off to fight them Yankees all by yo'self." His mother said, with pride in her voice, "Now, Louie, you stop foolin with Bubba, he had business to take care of. Come on ovah here, son, so I can fix you somethin to eat. I know you must be starvin to death cause you was gone befoe breakfast time." He looked at all the tempting food on the table and realized just how hungry he was. Hattie appeared out of nowhere and said, "Let me fix it for him, Miss Alice, you just sit there and relax yo'self, you been cookin all mornin." Hattie started heaping food on the plate, and when she handed it to him their eyes met and seemed to lock. He could not bring himself to stop staring at her. She had the most beautiful eyes he'd ever seen, big and brown; a man could just drown himself in them. The white dress she wore set off her pretty brown skin, and did justice to her small fine figure, while her neatly combed, short brown hair, had the fragrant smell of flowers. He took the plate and sat down quickly. This close encounter unnerved him to the point that his legs began to feel shaky.

Bubba noticed a strange-looking smile on Hattie's mama's face; it was like she knew something he didn't. He must make a conscious effort not to look at Hattie with a yearning that was difficult to hide. Miss Martha said, "Bubba ,I been thankin bout you and my daughter." His heart seem to jump up in his mouth, but he managed to say, "Which daughter, Miss Martha?" That reply caused everyone at the table to start laughing. "Boy, don't you play me for no fool, you know darn well which daughter; the one that got you trippin over your own feet. We may be old, but we ain't crazy. How ya'll young folks think you got here, anyways? Our men use to give us them dreamy-eyed looks too; next thang we knowed, we was buck naked with our legs open and nine months later here ya'll come." Bubba was so shocked by her frankness that he was speechless. Louie started to speak, most likely seeing a great opportunity for one of his jokes, but before he could utter a word she said, "Shut up Louie, I'm talkin now!" Hattie stood there looking at her mama just as dumbfounded as Bubba, afraid to say a word. "Now, like I was sayin, we know that you been sweet on Hattie for a long time now, and they ain't no doubtin that she want you for her man. When your mama and I first talked bout what we seen was happenin with you two, I told her that she was too young for you. The only reason I ain't said nothin to you befoe now is cause you been a real gentleman and never tried to force yo'self on her. I could tell that you really loved her and would nevah do nothin to brang harm to her. In time, I thought she would grow out of it and start flirtin with boys her own age, but I can see that ain't gonna happen. I guess thangs just work out for the best when you let the Lord do the thinkin. Your mama and me sort of looked at thangs a bit different today; with the war comin on and all. It seem to us like time ain't gone wait on nobody and young folks gone have to grow up sooner then they posed to. If somethin should happen to me on account of this war, I was figurin that it would be a comfortin thought to know that Hattie had a strong man to take care of her and protect her." She smiled at Bubba and said, "For the life of me I can't think of a better man than you, so I guess it would be alright if ya'll still have a mind to start courtin. Now, you remember I said start courtin; I ain't said nothin bout startin to make babies. You gits my meanin? Ya'll start out right and evahthang else will work out fine. You and Hattie can take them dumb looks off your faces and gone on over there and eat some of this good food." She turned to Louie and said, "Now what was you gone say?" "I ain't got nothin to say Martha, cause you done said it all." Then Louie broke out in a loud laugh that would have made the devil himself smile. While everyone at the table was having fun at their expense, Bubba and Hattie took their food with them, eased away, and went to a cozy spot nearer to the creek.

Bubba took Hattie's hand, held it gently, and told her how much he really did love her, and how he could not believe that in a matter of minutes, most of his dreams concerning her had come true. He could hardly wait for his final dream of marrying her to come to pass. Hattie leaned forward, gazing at him with those big dreamy eyes, and gave him a kiss, which set his heart to racing. "Bubba I know its gonna be hard for us not to come together as man and woman till we git married, but what mama said was right; we gonna have a whole lifetime of love makin and beautiful children to raise. This war won't last forevah and we all are gonna come through it just fine." Bubba, not wanting to dampen her spirit concerning the war simply said, "You're probably right, Hattie, this war should be over in no time." Yet in his heart he knew the war would not be over quickly, and maybe even go on for years. He dare not tell her that everyone was not going to come through it, as she put it, 'just fine.' "Just think, Bubba, now we can see each other anytime we want; no more sneakin round just to be near one another." "Hattie, there is nothing I want more than to be with you all the time, and as you said, one day that will happen, but for now there is much work to be done.

Tomorrow we start clearing land in order to build the camp and training area we will need for the militia. All of us men will have very little time to spend with our women, and all of the men who join the militia will be confined to camp until the training is completed. It's going to be hard on all of us but without proper training we don't stand a chance of protecting our people and this land. Do you understand?" "Yes, Bubba, I understand, but I want you to know that when I wake up in the mornin my first thoughts are of you. I can hardly wait for the day to begin, just so I can get a look at you or talk to you or be near you. Even now, just thinkin bout not seein you evahday, is causin my body to ache, but I know in my heart that you feel the same. So for now, just take me in yours arms and hold me and we'll pretend just for a little while that there is no war. Let me enjoy this wonderful day."

CHAPTER TEN

Bubba was up before dawn the next day full of energy and eager to get started on the projects at hand. He completed his team assignments and gave considerable thought to how he would tackle the job ahead; there was very little room for error because this camp had to be completed in record time. He knew that Bill was counting heavily on him and he had no intention of letting him down. He wondered if things were going smoothly for Bill in Folsom. There was room for doubt in his mind that things would go just as Bill had planned, because there was bound to be a diehard bigot who was surely planning to make as much trouble as he could and stir up hatred among his people.

Bubba realized that winning his fellow slaves over was nothing compared to what he would face in dealing with the white officers in the militia. They might accept him as an officer in charge of only the black troops, but he knew without question that he would have to prove himself capable of leadership many times just to be tolerated. He vowed to himself that he would stay focused on what he had to do and not let the racial slurs or derogatory remarks get to him; he would not give them the satisfaction of seeing him fall apart under pressure. Bubba decided that he must somehow instill this attitude in his men; they, too, would be subjected to ridicule. He heard a noise and looked around to see his mother coming into the kitchen. "Mama, what are you doing up so early? It's not even daybreak yet." "I figured you'd be up befoe dawn, son, and I'm not gonna let you leave here this mornin without havin a good breakfast. I know you got a lot on your mind and rightly so, but don't let the problems facin you put gray hair in yo head. Take them on one at a time and you'll do just fine. Now let me get started on breakfast for you befoe Hattie comes over here and beats me to it." They both had a good laugh at that one.

As Bubba was leaving the cabin he saw Sammy walking towards him. "Good morning, Bubba. Figures I'd stop by and walk over to the big house with you. The men should be gettin there pretty soon; those who ain't still drunk from all that free homebrew yestiday. I show have to say what a fine time I had. Man, I ate so much food it's a wonder my stomach didn't pop wide open. Yeah, everyone had a good time, even Meathead. Oops, I mean Meatball," and Sammy began laughing at his own joke. Bubba looked at him and smiled, while shaking his head. "Please don't make me have to fight that man again, cause I don't think he'd take too kindly to having his ass whipped twice in the same week." He had forgotten that when Sammy got to laughing so hard, he could be heard near and far, and always drew attention on the plantation. Bubba put his hand over his mouth to shut him up, while laughing and saying at the same time, "Come on, Sammy, we got to be serious this morning." Sammy finally calmed down as they approached the big house, and as the other men came into view, he looked as serious as an undertaker. The men had a "what the hell is goin on" look on their faces, but nobody said a word. Sammy was well known for pulling practical jokes on people and having a great sense of humor, but he was also known for being a man you could count on when the going got rough. When Bubba came closer to the big house he realized that the look of "what the hell is going on," on the faces of the men, was not caused by Sammy's antics, but because there was a young white man standing on the front porch, dressed in the uniform of an army officer. It was gray in color, instead of the blue he had become accustomed to seeing on his rare trips to Folsom. He concluded that the South had chosen this color to distinguish them from the Northern soldiers. Bubba could sense that this situation would spell trouble if not handled properly. He eased his way to the front of the men just as the officer was asking, "Who's in charge when Mr. Shields is away?" Bubba hadn't heard Bill's surname used in so long it took him a moment to realize that the soldier was referring to Bill. Everyone turned and looked at Bubba, but before he could answer, the soldier said, "No, I don't want to speak to the slave you've chosen as your spokesman; where is your overseer? Surely there must be a white man in charge during your master's absence?"

Bubba knew he had to decide quickly if he was going to play the role of a passive slave or assert himself as their leader. Bubba thought how ironic that he had contemplated a situation like this just this morning, and now here it was staring him in the face, challenging him to live up to the commitments he'd made to himself. He replied, "Sir, I am in charge when Master Bill is away. How can I be of service to you?" The officer looked stunned. "You mean to tell me that a slave is second in command of this plantation?" "That's about the size of it, Sir. I've been Master Bill's manservant for a number of years, and I've also been trained to see to the smooth operation of this plantation in his presence or absence. You may be assured that I am quite competent to answer anything that you wish to inquire about." Both stunned and angry, the officer said, "This must be some kind of joke, and in bad taste I might add. Now, boy, you tell me where

Mr. Shield's overseer is right now or I'll beat the tar out of you. I've never heard of a plantation without an overseer, and I'm beginning to think that you're one of them educated Yankee black bastards that army headquarters said would be coming down South to get you slaves to revolt against us." Bubba took a long, hard look at the officer, who was about two inches shorter than he was, but shared a similar, strong build that rivaled his own. If trouble came this man's way, Bubba felt certain he could handle it and then some. Long, straight sleek black hair, stopping just short of his shoulders, complemented the thin, neatly trimmed mustache he wore with quiet assurance. The officer's hooded, piercing eyes could spit blue sparks, yet also announced uneasiness he couldn't quite hide. Whatever else Bubba might discover about this man, he already knew one thing for sure; he would want him on his side. Bubba looked the officer straight in the eye, and said, "With all due respect, Sir, my skin may be black but I am not a bastard. And I am not a boy but the man who is going to beat the hell out of you if you continue to insult me." The officer looked at Bubba and could see that he meant every word he said. His first instinct was to reach for his revolver, but after looking at the angry faces of the other slaves, he thought better of it. He was thinking that he would probably be able to shoot one or two, but would soon be overpowered and beaten to death. Never in his life had a slave talked to him in this manner, and as he looked out into the crowd of men, all he saw was a sea of black; not one white man to come to his aid. He decided that this was truly a time for discretion to be the better part of valor.

Bubba said, "Now soldier, how about you answering some questions? Who are you and what do you want here?" "I am Lieutenant Roach, a proud soldier in the army of the Confederate States of America. I am here to help Mr. Shields form and train the new militia unit." "Then you should know that it's no longer Mister but Captain Shields, and in answer to your question, he's in Folsom making arrangements for our supplies to be transported here and to receive his orders. My name is Malachi, but most people call me Bubba. I'm going to be Captain Shield's aide in charge of the black soldiers, so I believe that makes us even in rank. Perhaps I'll look more convincing in uniform." The lieutenant, still looking bewildered, said, "Headquarters did not inform me that there would be a black officer in the ranks." Bubba said with a smile, "I know you don't like it, Lieutenant, but that's the way it is. You're looking at part of the men that are going to be in that militia. We're going to stand shoulder to shoulder with your men to protect our land." The only words the Lieutenant could find to say were, "Well, I'll be damned." Bubba replied, "My orders are to get the land cleared and work toward getting the camp completed as soon as possible. That's why you see all these men gathered here this morning; time won't wait on us so we must get started at once. Believe me when I say that I know all this comes as a shock to you, and it's hard to digest all of this at one time, but if you give us a chance, we'll grow on you. You might even start referring to us as men instead of boys. If your superior had properly informed you, we would not have gotten off to such a bad start. If we can now put that aside and pull together to get this job done, I have no doubt that the Army and Captain Shields would appreciate it. You've probably never seen, let alone talked to, an intelligent black man so I can understand your taking offense at my assertive behavior towards you. Consider that I am following orders just as you are; which means like it or not, we're stuck with each other. This unit is being formed with the blessing of some powerful people who can add more gold braid to your uniform or take some away; the choice is yours. Captain Shields will be returning by week's end, and he'll answer all those questions that are running around in your head right now. In the meantime, we could sure use your help, if you would be gracious enough to give it."

Lt. Roach couldn't believe what was happening to him. Everything that he had been taught as a child about slaves, formed his attitude toward them in his adult life. Never had he entertained the thought that they could think and make decisions by themselves, let alone be literate. He'd always regarded them as one step above animals, just as his father had taught him; which meant that they were able to think only well enough to do his bidding. He admitted to himself that this slave, Bubba, was right about his having never seen or talked to an intelligent, educated slave; let alone one who seemed to have a command of the English language that equaled his own. In a matter of minutes, this slave had sent everything he'd ever been taught (regarding slaves) crashing down around him, and for some strange reason he found it fascinating. Headquarters had given him the impression that they were being forced to fight. What Southerner (or Yankee for that matter) in his wildest dreams would ever consider that some slaves would regard this land as their home, and willingly fight the very people coming to free them. This was truly amazing! He then began thinking selfishly of how his helping to complete this mission would do wonders for his career. In an effort to restore his dignity he said, "Yes, I will help you, but only on condition that you listen to me and do what I say because of my experience in these matters. When Captain Shields returns I'll be able to confirm your story. If he doesn't return by week's end and confirm it as you say, I'll bring the wrath of the entire Confederate Army down on your head." Bubba answered his challenge. "I understand exactly, Lieutenant. Now let's get on with the business at hand. Then I'll show you to the guest room and arrange for some breakfast; I'm sure you must be hungry and tired after your long trip. One of my men will see to your horse." He turned toward the men and said, "For those of you that could not hear or don't understand what's going on, this is Lieutenant Roach. He was sent here to help us with our preparations, which includes your military training. Please do everything you can to make him feel welcome. Let's prove to him that with proper training we're gonna make damn good soldiers." Most of the men cheered, but some of them didn't know what to make of this white man in the odd clothes; they had never seen an army uniform. Bubba escorted Lt. Roach into the house, telling him that he would return later in the day after the Lieutenant had eaten and rested, and take him out to the future campsite.

When Bubba finally returned to the men they greeted him with loud applause and cheers. Meatball stepped to the front and said, "Bubba, we never thought that any of us would live to see the day when a slave would stand up to a white man like you did and get away with it; you made us real proud. If you want to lead us straight to hell, we gone follow you cause by the time you finish talkin to the Devil, he'll be askin God to please come and take these fools outa here befoe they sets fire to theyselves."

After the laughter died down, he thanked them for their pledge of loyalty and said, "Now men, I've broken you up into three work teams. Arthur and David will take charge of the men who will be clearing the land. Sammy will head up the team that will do the actual building of the camp. When we finish clearing the land, more of you will be assigned to Sammy to help speed up the building work, and the rest of you will be given other duties. Meatball will oversee all three teams, which means that he will be responsible for keeping everything on track (Bubba could have sworn that he saw Meatball's head swell at hearing this!). Please listen for your names as I call them out, and after you've all been assigned, we'll load the wagons and head on out; we've already lost some time this morning so we'll have to make it up."

As they approached the location, Bubba visualized the camp upon completion, and decided that this land was indeed the perfect spot. As the wagons came to a stop, he jumped down and began to help the men unload the equipment. He was thankful that there were not a lot of trees to contend with, but there was a heck of a lot of brush and weeds, and the land would have to be leveled out. However, the woods behind the camp would give them a good supply of firewood and also serve as an excellent training area. Turning to his three leaders he said, "Arthur, take your team and start to work on the left; David, start on the right. Sammy, you can split your team into two groups, coming in behind the other teams and leveling the ground as they move forward. I've drawn up a rough plan of where the main camp is to be located and what it should look like, but feel free to make any changes that you think are necessary. When it comes to building something, you're the expert and I'm relying on your good judgment. The only thing I'm sure of is that we'll have at least three hundred men who will be housed in tents. Meatball, are you ready to get to work?" "Bubba, you know that I stays ready. Okay men, you heard what the man said, let's git to work."

Bubba's thoughts again turned to Bill. He figured things must be going according to plan, otherwise they would not have sent Lieutenant Roach from Army Headquarters to help them out. However, Bill's not returning as scheduled, would probably spook the officer enough to have him riding to headquarters screaming slave revolt! All Bill would find when he did return would be all of us hanging from trees! Bubba finally decided to put those thoughts out of his head and concentrate on his own responsibilities. Thinking about hanging from a tree wasn't a thought he wanted to dwell upon!

Bubba worked with the men for several hours. Man was it hot! He finally shouted, "Men, let's take a break in the shade of those trees over there, and take our food and some water with us; ain't no sense in us falling out in this heat." Louie shouted, "Thank you, Jesus! For a minute there I thought Bubba was tryin to kill his daddy so's he could git the fortune I'm gone leave him." Needless to say, that brought a cackle from everyone. Bubba decided that after he'd eaten and rested awhile, it was time to go back and get Lieutenant Roach.

CHAPTER ELEVEN

As Bill entered the town of Folsom, he found the situation pretty much as he suspected. Soldiers were everywhere, prancing around as if they were invincible, bands were playing and patriotic Southern songs filled the air. If he didn't know better, he'd swear the circus was in town. He was pretty tired after the two-hour ride to town, and decided to stick to his plan to seek out (as Bubba would say), his lady friend. He hoped he would not run into any of the town officials and be forced to join in the festivities; there would be plenty of time for that. Pulling up at the livery stable, he asked the man to tend to his horse. He then walked until he came to a cute little house that sat back off the main street, with a yard that was quite pretty, and overflowing with flowers. He knocked on the door and when it opened, a woman pretty enough to take your breath away, stood smiling at him. Hat in hand, Bill said, "Excuse me, Miss, but could you tell me where a man could get a decent bath around here and possibly get laid in the process?" She laughed lightly, replying, "Come on in, Sir, I think that perhaps I can arrange something on that order."

Several hours later as they lay in each other's arms she said, "Bill, everyone knows that I am your bought and paid for whore, and maybe they have a right to say that. After all, you bought this house and give me everything I need to have a comfortable life here. They refer to me as your "lady friend," as if I don't have a name, and everyone knows you are the only man in my life. I just want you to know that even without all the trimmings I would be yours, because money can't buy the deep love that I have for you." Bill looked into her eyes and spoke softly. "Now Mona, you aren't going to get all teary-eyed on me are you?" "No, I am not, but sometimes I get to thinking of how nice it would be to have you here with me all the time, instead of just your once a week visits." "Mona, are you having second thoughts about our relationship?" "The only second thoughts I'm having is that I should have gone for the grand prize and gotten you to marry me instead of settling for being your whore-in-waiting; we really could have a great life together. You're probably thinking that it's one thing to sleep with a whore, but only a fool would marry one. I know the men that attend church every Sunday after spending most of Saturday night at the local whorehouse would be astounded, and the good ladies of the town would probably have to be sedated if we were to marry. I think they would come around to accepting me, in time, not as one of them, but as your wife; which is all I desire. And with the war starting, people are going to be too concerned with their own lives to spend time or lose sleep thinking about us." Bill looked thoughtful at this disclosure. "So, is it because of the war that you are choosing to tell me your true feelings?" "It must be, Bill, because the thought of something happening to you or you possibly being killed scares me so much. It makes me want to share all my life with you, as your lover, and your loving wife."

Bill gave Mona a long hard look. "You've heard, haven't you?" "Yes, Bill, I know that you'll be commanding the militia that's been assigned to defend this area and I hate to even think about it. I may be a woman but we both know I'm not a stupid one; we can imagine that if the Yankees decide to march on Folsom, they'll run over you like you weren't even there." "No, sweetheart; our job is only to hold them until the main force arrives. With proper training, when the time comes, we will be able to do just that. We both know we just can't stand by and do nothing; we have to make preparations for the defense of Folsom, and men are going to die in that effort." With tears in her eyes, Mona whispered, "I just pray to God, Bill, that you won't be one of them." "And so do I, Mona. As far as you and I are concerned, I care for you a great deal, and if I were to be honest with myself that caring could even be love. But in the coming months none of us will have much time for romance. But sweetheart, I promise you that when this war is over I'll strongly consider making an "honest" woman of you; if you think you could really stand putting up with my snoring every night instead of once a week." She laughed, tenderly touching his cheek. "I could put up with it for a lifetime, my love."

After Mona finally succumbed to sleep, Bill headed straight for the Mayor's office where he knew "everyone who was anyone" in the town would be gathered. He had no doubt that some would be sporting their new tailor-made gray uniforms and giving their rendition of mock battles, naturally with the South being the obvious victor. When he entered the office, sure enough there stood the Mayor in his entire splendor, wearing a magnificent uniform that said, "I am a proud Major in the Confederate Army of the South," giving his version of the outcome of the war. His aides and lieutenants were gathered around him listening as if they were hanging onto every word he spoke. It looked to Bill like practicing the art of ass kissing was getting off to an early start. When the Mayor finished giving his scenario he greeted Bill warmly and called for everyone's attention.

"Well, as you can see gentlemen, the man of the hour has finally arrived. Some of you gentlemen from headquarters have never had the pleasure, so let me introduce you to Captain Shields, the man who came up with the plan for the defense of Folsom and who will be commanding the newly formed militia unit. As most of you already know, this unit will consist of volunteers only, mostly loyal slaves. Of course, they will have white sergeants and officers to train and lead them; I tell you this plan was a stroke of genius. I'd give anything to see the look on the faces of those damn Yankees when they come face to face with those slaves wearing Confederate uniforms and shooting at them; it just makes me feel good all over." After the laughter died down, one officer said, "Well, if you can train a monkey, I see no reason why we can't train a slave. Of course we'll have to keep a large supply of bananas on hand." The whole room erupted with laughter; Bill held his contempt for this officer and his remark in check, knowing that he could not afford to make enemies; at least for now. Bill forced a smile and said, "Yes, I am sure that the Yankees will be quite astonished; and I don't believe we've been introduced." "Begging your pardon Sir, I am Lieutenant Wells. I volunteered and have been assigned to your unit. As a matter of fact, there is a Lieutenant Roach who's also been assigned but his orders were to report directly to you at your plantation, and he should be arriving there by tomorrow morning. A message was to be sent informing you of his pending arrival, but things are pretty hectic at headquarters, as you can well understand. However, I'm sure that your overseer can accommodate him until your return. You'll find him to be a capable officer; he'll have those blacks whipped into shape in short order." While still smiling at his little joke, he went on to say, "My orders called for me to leave a day earlier and report directly to the Major, and deliver the important dispatches into his hands. After accomplishing that, I am to put myself at your disposal Captain, in the form of an Aide."

Bill felt his dislike for this officer growing by the minute, but he said, "I am sure that you also will be an asset to the unit (mentally substituting the word ass). We'll talk again when I've finished consulting with the Major." Bill watched Lt. Wells as he strutted around the room, reminding him of a puffed-up bantam rooster. His mouth was constantly overloading his very narrow ass. Five-foot-six-inches tall, he was the perfect caricature; a short man needing to believe he was nevertheless the equivalent of a Goliath. Bill doubted if he weighed even one hundred forty pounds soaking wet. His pale, washed-out complexion only accentuated his ghostly gray eyes that seemed to be constantly darting around, sizing up the situation, and plotting how to use it to his advantage. Bill could almost feel slyness oozing out of every pore, surrounding him like a dark, slippery cloak. And despite the fiery red color of his hair and handlebar mustache, he did not generate heat, but its opposite, a deadly cold presence. Bill instinctively knew that Lt. Wells was a man not to be trusted, and if ever given any real power, he would prove to be a cunning and dangerous enemy. After being formally introduced to the rest of the officers, who were assigned to the regular army and Cavalry, the Major asked him to step into his private office so they could confer with each other in private. As they entered the room, Bill could not help noticing several army uniforms neatly laid out on the couch. The Major said, "Knowing how cramped your schedule is, I took the liberty of having your tailor make them for you. I hope you don't take offense?" "Certainly not. In fact I'm pleased that you were so thoughtful, and to be honest with you, that little detail had completely slipped my mind. It's going to take awhile for me to make the adjustment from civilian to soldier, so I ask you to please bear with me." "Don't worry yourself about that, Captain, most of us are in the same boat, but I'm sure we'll get the hang of it in no time."

Bill took in the appearance of the Major; his rotund face was red and sweaty, and his extremely small brown eyes seemed squeezed into place, with a shifty look about them. By Bill's estimation, he was about 5'9" tall, and approaching 300 pounds. The Major's portly body carried most of its weight in his protruding stomach and generous backside. What was left of his thinning brown hair, looked like a pathetic, threadbare carpet. The Major looked like a dressed up hog in fancy uniform. Bill couldn't help but laugh inwardly at this comic figure.

"I can sense that you have something on your mind, Captain, would you like to share it with me?" Managing to keep a straight face, Bill looked the Major in the eye, saying, " I know that it's customary for a commanding officer to choose his Aide, and I was just wondering why I was not given that opportunity?" "Army headquarters felt that you had little to choose from, and perhaps rightly so. Lieutenant Wells comes highly recommended by his superiors and you can rely upon him to keep these blacks in their place. He comes from a fine Southern family and knows firsthand how to deal with blacks when they get a little, shall we say, restless. If this should happen, some harsh consequences might have to be imposed; it would be good to have an officer at your disposal that can handle those situations for you. Don't you see, Captain, that way you get to keep your reputation among the slaves as a fine slave Master while Lieutenant Wells does your dirty work and none of them will be the wiser? After all, we certainly don't want them to get it in their heads that they're going to be just as good as white men when this war is over, now do we?" The Major's words filled Bill with anger; he could feel his blood to begin to boil. It took all the strength Bill could muster, to say, "We certainly don't, Sir, but Major, do you think it sound to build this unit on a foundation based on fear?" "You know as well as I do, Captain, that their fear of us is the only thing that keeps us from being slaughtered in our sleep." "But, Major, these slave volunteers are the ones that are loyal to us, as we all agreed in our last meeting." "Yes, Captain, I still agree, but that loyalty exists only because they've never had a taste of power and we don't intend to give it to them. I am sure you see my point?" "Yes, Sir, I most certainly do, and I intend to take full advantage of your experience in these matters." Although Bill found the words he had just uttered to the Major repugnant, he had to face the reality of the situation, and not let his personal feelings get in the way of achieving his ultimate goal. The Major, noticing that Bill seemed a little edgy, said, "Captain, you seem to be a little nervous, are you having any doubts, concerning the use of our slaves to help fight this war?" Bill quickly responded, "Definitely not, Major!" "Splendid! Now that we agree on that issue, Captain, we must move on to other matters."

Bill was thinking about the promise he made to Bubba, and now was as good a time as any to approach the subject and make an attempt to put him in good standing with the Major. He had to pull this off without drawing suspicion. "There is just one more thing, Major. Do you remember my manservant Bubba?" "Of course I do, he's a fine example of a slave who knows his place and is fiercely loyal to you." "You're exactly right on both counts, Sir, and that is why I wish to put him in charge of the black soldiers. Of course he would be subordinate to any white officer in rank. Bubba would be of tremendous value serving as our eyes and ears among them; they trust him completely, and that would definitely work to our advantage. Giving him the rank of lieutenant, and having him answerable only to me, would give these slave soldiers a sense of security that may stop any thoughts of rising up against us. We'll do as we've always done, pit them against each other; the poor fools won't even realize they have a Judas among them. That policy has worked in the past and it will work now; I just thank God they've never had the brains to figure it out." "Captain, you constantly amaze me with your ability to think things through and come up with sound ideas. And this one is excellent." The Major smiled wickedly as he said, "Bubba would rather cut off his own nuts before he would betray you. Consider it done, Captain."

Bill forced out the words, "Thank you, sir," while feeling sick to his stomach playing the roll of a co-conspirator with this unscrupulous bastard, but at least now the cards were on the table and their hands were exposed. He now knew with certainty that the Major and most of the officers gathered here had no intention of rewarding the slaves for putting their lives on the line in the defense of the South. However, he still felt strongly that such an act of patriotism on their part would cause the decent people of the South to take a hard look at the possibility of slave reform. Bill saw his duty as both leader and protector, knowing the cruelty some Southern masters could inflict on their slaves, showing no compassion or understanding.

"Now, Captain, most of your supplies will be loaded onto wagons by Thursday. At that time, a small force of volunteer white soldiers are due to arrive; mostly corporals and sergeants from the regular army. These men will be invaluable to you in the areas of training and instilling discipline in the slaves. Naturally, they are not to be quartered with the blacks, but close enough to keep an eye on them. Provided we don't encounter any complications, you should be able to start back by Friday morning. The other plantation owners assured me that their slave volunteers could be made ready to leave that very morning. Your sergeant can pick them up on the way to your plantation training grounds. The way I figure it, you'll have about two hundred or so black soldiers under your command. We estimate that it will take about six weeks to get them trained and ready to fight. The slaves' uniforms won't be ready for at least a month; you know we have to outfit our white soldiers first. I'll leave instructions to have someone inform you as soon as they arrive." "Leave instructions, Major?" Bill asked, puzzled. "Yes, Captain, I'm being assigned to General Lee." "Congratulations, Major, that is quite an honor." "Thank you, Captain, I am truly grateful to have this chance to prove myself worthy of command." As he said this, Bill thought, I'm truly grateful to have one less problem to worry about, while he said out loud, "I have no doubt that you will do yourself proud, Major."

After asking Lieutenant Wells to join them, the Major discussed the strategy Army Headquarters intended to use in the defense of Folsom. He spoke for a considerable amount of time. Finally, the Major said, "Gentlemen, I suggest we call it a night and start again first thing in the morning; sharper minds will leave less room for error. Captain Shields, I'll expect to see you in uniform tomorrow. Your days of being a civilian have ended." Bill responded with a quiet, "Yes, Sir. Goodnight, gentlemen." After Bill left the room, the Major turned to Lieutenant Wells and said, "The man must take me for a complete fool. I know he is loyal to the South without question, but I am also aware of his desire for slave reform. Lucky for him that he stops just short of being seen as an abolitionist; if he didn't have such powerful friends in high places, I would gladly expose him. Little does he know that this plan of his to defend Folsom with slave soldiers has played right into my hands. My sources tell me that he dreams of the day when slaves will be freed by the South, and he's completely sold on the idea that this act of patriotism on their part will help to hasten that day. You can be damn sure I'll do everything within my power to make certain that never happens! Now, Lieutenant, you and I can discuss the real plan; using his group of slaves as our sacrificial lambs. We will leak false information to the Yankees, leading them to believe we have a significant force here, that's totally unprepared for an attack. Hopefully, they will see this as a chance to claim a great victory and decide to have a regiment march on Folsom. We'll allow them to pass right through without any interference; this tactic should boost their confidence. Once they start the attack on Folsom, we won't intervene until we're satisfied that most of the defenders have been killed. We'll use the South Carolina regiments to attack them from all sides, and cut off any chance of escape. The element of surprise will work like a charm; we'll send them straight to hell. Picture it, Lieutenant! I can see those Yankee soldiers, begging to surrender. We will have struck a major blow to the Yankees. This action will throw the North into a panic, especially when the public finds out that the very people they came to free, were among the first ones to shoot at them. Something tells me that their idealistic views on slavery will be badly shaken. So, Lieutenant Wells, train them so that they can die well. Just remember that as soon as these soldiers have been trained to your satisfaction, you and Lieutenant Roach are to report back to headquarters. We certainly cannot afford to lose two fine officers, and you'll be supplied with pre-written orders permitting you to do so." "I understand completely, Major," Lt. Wells said with a sly look, "but what about the white soldiers?" "Let them perish with the others; they're nothing but white trash anyway, which makes them expendable. Do we understand each other?" "Yes sir," Lt. Wells said, smartly saluting, "You know you can depend on me to carry out my orders to the letter."

It was late in the evening when Bill headed back to Mona; he wanted to be with her as much as possible, knowing that every minute spent in her arms would be a comfort. He was also eager to partake of his favorite meal, which she always prepared when he came to visit. Bill could picture her slicing that scrumptious-looking roast beef and putting it on his plate, right next to a huge pile of mashed potatoes, and topping the whole thing off with thick brown gravy. He quickened his pace; just thinking about it made his hunger more urgent. As Bill walked along, he wondered how Bubba was coping with Lieutenant Roach. He wished now that he had delayed his departure for one more day so that he would have been there to greet this officer and given him specific orders curtailing his authority until he returned from Folsom. Bill knew that the officer would be outraged at finding a slave in charge of the plantation during his absence, and from what Lieutenant Wells said about him, that information would immediately call for a confrontation with Bubba. Bill decided that he must leave Folsom by Friday morning at all costs; he'd leave right now if he were not tied to the military. The urge to come to the aid of his friend was strong, but he reminded himself that Bubba was quite good at handling delicate situations, even when it came to bigots. Bill had seen the aggressive side of Bubba only once, and that was during a dinner party when a male guest had a few drinks too many and began using vulgar language in the presence of the ladies. After Bill had asked his guest to leave, he became belligerent. Bill remembered Bubba suddenly stepping in between the two of them, looking the man straight in the eyes, and saying, "Sir, my Master says its time for you to leave; do you wish to do so with or without my assistance?" The man took one look at Bubba, and made a hasty exit to the door. And so, Bill thought, Bubba would be quite capable of handling this unforeseen situation. The only thing he really had to worry about was whether or not the Lieutenant would still be standing when he returned. He smiled to himself and set his mind to other matters.

There was something about the way the Major was so quick to agree with his suggestions that bothered him. He wondered if there could be some other motive for wanting this plan to form a militia consisting of slaves, to succeed. He also questioned the two Lieutenants that Army Headquarters chose to send, because he just could not picture them volunteering for such a mission. His suspicions led him to believe that there was definitely something he was not being told. Maybe he was being a bit paranoid; they probably decided that the success of a mission like this would help to further their careers. He was sure that the truth would come out eventually, and he just hoped that it wouldn't be too late to do anything about it, if it turned out to be a threat to his men.

After a memorable evening with Mona, Bill arose early the next morning and headed for what was now the Major's office. When he walked in, the junior officers in the room saluted him, and the Major said, "Well, Captain, I must say that you strike a fine pose in that uniform." As Bill was saluting he couldn't help thinking...all this saluting, yes sir, no sir, Major this, Lieutenant that, was beginning to get on his damn nerves! It felt like he wasn't a real person anymore. Nevertheless, he spoke the required, "Thank you, Sir."

CHAPTER TWELVE

The trip back to the plantation gave Bubba time to reflect on the situation he now found himself in, with the sudden appearance of Lt. Roach. It was without question that he'd have to walk a fine line with him; convincing him that he was only following the orders of his Master, and not a slave drunk with the power that was given to him, was imperative. As he approached the house, he made a decision to take the approach of a slave who's become overwhelmed with responsibilities and needs the help of a white man to guide him through the decision-making process. This would surely feed Lt. Roach's ego enough to buy the time he needed until Bill's return.

As he was about to enter the house, he saw Hattie off in the distance waving at him. He threw her a kiss and continued on his way; this was definitely not the time for romance. He found Lt. Roach in the dining room; the cook had just prepared lunch for him. He looked up at Bubba and said, "As soon as I've finished my meal we'll go and take a look at this land that you claim is the perfect spot for the camp." "I'm certainly glad that you're willing to do this, Sir. You see, I really don't feel comfortable with making these important decisions when there is a fine white gentlemen like yourself available who is much more qualified to do so. I wouldn't dare say this in front of the other slaves, but when I said we needed your help this morning, the truth is, I need it desperately. I don't want to disappoint Master Bill, but I think he's given me more to do than I can mentally handle." Bubba could tell that he had struck the right chord when the Lieutenant said, "Very well Bubba, I'm doing this against my better judgment, but it's good to hear that you've come to your senses. I will stand in your Master's place and help you, but as I told you this morning, if he doesn't return by Friday before sundown there will be hell to pay. Don't worry, I won't embarrass you in front of your fellow slaves. Do we have an understanding?" "Yes sir, we sure do." Lt. Roach knew that Bubba was playing him for a fool; however, he decided to play along until he could sort things out.

He was lost in his own thoughts as Bubba drove the wagon back to the campsite. He had jumped at the chance to further his career by signing up for the original plan intended for this militia unit. However, since that time this scheme that headquarters and the Major had come up with, was laying heavy on his heart. Although he had agreed to participate, the thought of allowing hundreds of soldiers to be slaughtered was now beginning to eat at him. Knowing that they were not, and would not be considered as equals, these slaves were still choosing to fight for the South. Somehow Bubba had sparked an interest to do something he'd never done before; look at them as human beings.

The men were hard at work when they arrived. Lt. Roach thought it impressive how well the slaves seemed to be working together, especially considering the fact it was being done without the supervision of an overseer. In one voice they were all singing a song whose rhythm matched the rhythm of their common labors. As a young boy and even now as a man, he found it amazing how slaves could perform backbreaking chores and make it seem like fun through their music. He recalled watching his father's slaves work in this manner, and sometimes felt the urge to join them in their singing, but he knew his father would not only disapprove, he would have beaten the hell out of him. He had never questioned why slaves had to be treated so inhumanely; he had just accepted his father's teachings as gospel. He suddenly realized this was a golden opportunity for him to explore the minds of these slaves and interact with them in any way he chose to. After all, there wasn't another white man around for miles, and Captain Shields wouldn't be returning until Friday; who would be the wiser? Now was the chance for him to satisfy that little boy's inquisitiveness, and by God he would do it. With a knowing look in his eye he turned to Bubba and said, "I know that you were trying to manipulate me this afternoon with that, "Please help me, Master," speech of yours. I must admit that was a pretty good show you put on. So, what do you say we stop this game playing and simply work together?" Bubba smiled and said, "Well, I guess you got me on that one, and it would be a relief not to have power struggles between us; of course I agree." Bubba held out his hand, which the Lieutenant just looked at for a few seconds, while thinking that today was surely bringing about a lot of firsts in his life. He said, "Bubba, I suppose it would be alright for you to call me Richard, seeing that as you so aptly put it, we're equal in rank." Finally, he took Bubba's hand, and unknowingly to either one of them, began a friendship that would be called upon in the not too distant future.

Bubba showed him where he thought the main camp should be located and told him of his plans for the wooded area. Lt. Roach agreed with him, but offered a few suggestions that made good sense.

Bubba took off his shirt and said, "We have only a few hours of daylight left, so I'm going to lend the men a hand." Lt. Roach decided that it was "now or never" as he walked over to the wagon, took off his shirt and laid it neatly on the seat. Grabbing an ax, he walked back to where Bubba was standing and quietly said, "Now, where do we start?" Suddenly they both became aware of the complete silence that surrounded them; all work and singing had stopped as the men gazed at Lt. Roach in a state of stupefaction. He looked at the men, saying, "What's the matter? Haven't you seen a white man with his shirt off and an ax in his hand before?" Louie spoke up, saying, "Yeah Suh, but that's always been a sign for anythang black to start runnin like hell." The men erupted in laughter as they returned to their work and rhythmic singing. Richard, not knowing the words started humming along as Bubba just looked at him, a big grin on his face. The sun was beginning to set when Bubba called to Richard (who just happened to be working alongside Meatball) and said, "I think we've done a good day's work, what do you say we call it a day?" "You're absolutely right, Bubba. At the rate we're going we'll have this land cleared by tomorrow this time." Meatball, in a respectful tone, turned to the Lieutenant and said, "Beggin your pardon, Suh, but you work pretty good for a white man." Realizing this was a compliment, Richard replied, "But I'm no match for you men when it comes to hard work. Can you show me an easier way to use this ax tomorrow?" Meatball hardly knew what to say. No white man had ever given him credit for havin sense nough to do nothin better than he could. He was thinkin bout how funny life could be; this mornin he was ready to break this man's neck, and now he wasn't show of what his feelins was, but he felt safe in sayin, "Yeah Suh, I'd be proud to show you."

As the men started putting their tools back on the wagons, Bubba called Sammy, David and Arthur over and introduced them to Richard as the crew bosses. Then he turned to Richard and said, "The man whose respect you seem to have won is called Meatball, and please don't ask me why." Richard started laughing because that was exactly what he was thinking. Bubba shared his laugh, saying, "Meatball is the foreman and the man responsible for keeping all the work teams operating smoothly."

The men were anxious for a hot bath and a good meal after a day of sweat-popping work, so they wasted no time in starting back. As the wagon rolled along, Bubba turned to Richard and said, "May I ask you a personal question?" "Of course you can, Bubba, what is it?" "What in the hell happened to you today? I've never seen a man change so fast in my life." Richard gathered his thoughts before answering. "All my life I have been told what to think and how to think about it. To be honest with you, I've never before had the guts to break with family tradition and draw my own conclusions about your people. Once you find your comfort zone in life it's very difficult to do anything that might disturb it. Somehow you've managed to rekindle the desire I had as a boy to see your race in a different light, so now I'm simply taking advantage of this opportunity to do so. It's truly amazing what I've learned in just one day. That's given me pause to wonder how much I could learn in my lifetime." Bubba said, "You know, I read somewhere that once you stop looking at the race of a people and start to look at them as individuals that your life will be forever changed for the better. Apparently there must be something to that. Well, seeing that you're in such an inquisitive mood, how about sampling our native cooking tonight?" "Bubba, I'm inclined to take you up on that offer. Man, am I hungry! What's for supper?" "My Mama's specialty, neck bones and rice; you're in for real treat." Richard could not think of a suitable reply, and the look on his face said, "What in the hell have I let myself in for?" Bubba smiled and said, "Don't look so worried; they're really quite tasty and if you're lucky enough to get one with some meat on it, man you'll be in hog heaven." Richard finally managed to get out, "Did you say neck bones?" "I sure did! We'll be expecting you for supper, and I'll point out our cabin on the way in so you won't have any trouble finding it." Bubba was thinking, man, my daddy is sure gonna have him some fun tonight.

Everyone in Bubba's family made it a point to be at home for this momentous occasion; no one wanted to miss out on the opportunity of having a white man (other than Master Bill), sit down to supper with them. The whole slave quarter was buzzing with the news. Bubba was hoping that people wouldn't come over and start gawking at them through the window. Just as Mary finished preparing supper, a knock came at the door and suddenly you could have cut the silence with a knife. Bubba answered it and there stood Hattie. "Seein as how this is sorta a special occasion, I figure with me soon to be a part of your family and all, that it would be alright for me to invite myself to supper. It's alright, ain't it Bubba?" He was caught completely off guard. His mama seeing that he was in between a rock and a hard place, said, "Of course child, my future daughter-in-law is welcome here anytime." Before the door was tightly closed another knock came, and this time it was the man of the hour. Louie called, "Come on in, Master Richard, I ain't much on this yea military stuff, so's I figures it be alright foe me to call you, Master Richard, foe the time bein. Yo probably just as nervous as we is. Just think, this mornin I was thinkin bout makin you our supper, but you turnin out to be a fine gentleman. Come pull up a chair so's we can eat, cause that boy of mine done worked at least five pounds off me today." After being seated, he was introduced to each family member and Hattie. Everyone seemed to be a bit jittery. Richard decided to relieve the tension, by saying, "If my father could see me now, the first thing he would do is disown me and the second thing would be to hang all of you, so this meal better be as good as Bubba says it is, because if he finds out about this, I would at least like to be sent out into the world as a pauper on a full stomach." That remark brought a hearty laugh from everyone.

Alice sat a heaping plate of neck bones and rice in front of him, and Richard had to admit that it smelled delicious, although he was lost at how to go about eating them. Hattie spoke up and said, "Master Richard, you gone have to forgit bout all them fancy eatin habits; just pick them up with your hands, eat the meat and suck the juice off them bones like you mean business." No one else at the table made any remarks because they were busy doing exactly as Hattie had suggested. Richard picked one up and went to work; pretty soon his pile of cleaned bones was equal to everyone else at the table. When the supper was finished, he said, "Miss Alice, I've eaten superb meals all over this land and I must say that this one ranks up there with the best of them." With a twinkle and a smile, Louie pointed out, "And I believe that somebody in yo family was playin in the woodpile, cause you took to them bones like you was born to it." This started a lot of joking and laughter that went on into late evening, with the merriment ending only after they talked about the hard day's work ahead of them. While bidding everyone goodnight and thanking them for their hospitality, Richard felt as if he were saying goodnight to people he had known a lifetime. There was so much warmth and love in that cabin it was infectious; he was proud of himself for having found the courage to break with the bigoted beliefs of his family and make an attempt to see slaves as human beings. Lt. Roach would sleep well tonight.

The next few days were filled with hard, backbreaking work. They toiled from sunup to sundown giving careful attention to every detail. Their goal of completing the camp before Master Bill's return had been met; all that remained to be done was setting up the tents, which were included in the supplies he was bringing with him tomorrow. Bubba and Richard agreed that the men had done an excellent job and should be rewarded for doing so; that meant the homebrew would be flowing tonight.

Rubbing his weary shoulders, Bubba said, "I'm glad that tomorrow is Friday, not only because we've finished our tasks, but also so you'll finally know for sure that we brought no harm to Master Bill." "Bubba, I knew that after the first night I spent having supper with you and your family. Until now I would never have believed that such caring and loyalty could exist between a Master and his slaves. He must be an

Tommie Thompson

extremely fine man to deserve your unwavering trust in him." "Yes, he is Richard, and from where I stand, someday men will say the same of you. Now let's head on home so we can get cleaned up, eat us a fine meal and head on over to the barn." "To the barn?" Richard turned to Bubba and with a raised eyebrow asked, "Did you say barn, Bubba?" "Yes, to the barn, where most of the drinking, telling of tall tales and outright lies takes place around here. I sure hope you can hold your own; you should feel honored because Master Bill has been the only white man given that honor. Arthur came up to me today and said the men decided that as a man that's gotten down in the dirt and worked shoulder-to-shoulder with them, you've earned their respect and the right to join them, if you choose to." "I don't know what to say Bubba, except that I would be honored to join you."

Later that night, as Bubba entered the barn he paused, remembering happy times shared with family and friends in this old red barn with its white roof. This special refuge; a place where they could come to release their burdens, share their troubles and talk about the happier moments in their lives. He felt such nostalgia as the smells of sweat, hay and even horse manure brought memories he would never forget. He looked up at the loft, where none of the men sat at these gatherings. It was considered a place of honor, to be occupied only by the spirits of the men who had gathered here in past generations. Bubba could only hope this gathering would not be their last. And so it was that the slaves and one white man took turns telling lies and reliving outrageous deeds well into the night. Eventually the hard work of the day and the homebrew began to take its toll, and those who could speak coherently said their goodnights and slowly started towards the door; some walking, some being half carried, and some left on the barn floor; passed out cold.

Bubba woke up the next morning not even remembering his return trip to the cabin, let alone getting into bed. The sun was shinning through his window, telling him that he had slept way past the time he would normally get up. He jumped out of bed and found that except for his shoes, he was still fully clothed; man, he thought, I must have really tied one on last night. When he entered the kitchen, his father and brothers were sitting at the table just finishing up breakfast. Louie said, "Ain't no need to be hurryin to do nothin Bubba, since you wasn't round to tell us yo plans for today and seein that Master Bill won't be arrivin till sometime this afternoon, Master Richard told us to take the mornin off, cause there would be plenty of work for us to do with unloadin them wagons and all when he gits here. I tell you that man can show hold his liquor; he was the first one up this mornin. I think I might be right bout that wood pile," Louie said, chuckling to himself.

Bubba walked over to the big house, found Richard in the library, and thanked him for giving the men their instructions, complimenting him on his sound thinking. "Now tell me, if you can, how did I get home last night, because I can't remember a thing!" Richard smiled and said, "Your father and I half carried and dragged you; if a good time was had by anyone, it was certainly you. We decided to let you sleep late and get a much-needed rest; with Captain Shields returning today, you'll need all of your wits about you to help with the next phase of our project. For the record, I had a great time last night too, but everyone knew without saying, that the coming months will bring little cause or opportunity for celebration."

CHAPTER THIRTEEN

Bill was glad to be on the road back home. The days spent in Folsom had really taken a toll on him, not only did he have to put up with that idiot Lt. Wells during his stay there, he had to bring the bastard back with him. He thanked God that everything went as scheduled, allowing him to leave as planned; although the going would be slow on this return trip because of the heavy load the horses had to pull. However, even at that, they should make it home just before noon, barring any unforeseen complications. Most of the regular soldiers had already set out in empty wagons to pick up the volunteer slaves from the neighboring plantations and would transport them to the training camp. He hoped to have the tents set up before their arrival later in the day.

He figured that by now Bubba would be pacing the floor awaiting his arrival, if Lt. Roach hadn't already driven him to commit an act of murder. There was no doubt in his mind that the project he had entrusted Bubba with completing on time was done; just how he got it done with that Lieutenant breathing down his neck would be an interesting story.

Lieutenant Wells galloped up to Bill's wagon and said, "It's a shame that we won't have as much time as we counted on to train these boys, Captain." "Yes, Lieutenant, I quite agree, but the Yankees are on the move. It seems their desire to end this war as quickly as possible equals ours; somehow we must get these men prepared for battle in four weeks instead of the estimated time of six." "Don't worry Captain, I'll have them ready for you, believe me." However, Bill was worried, not about the men being ready for battle, but of the tactics this officer would employ to train them. He realized that Lt. Wells would have to be dealt with, but decided to carefully pick the place and time to do it. He smiled, thinking, there is nothing like a good old-fashioned ass whipping to help change a man's attitude; it was a tempting thought, but he hoped it wouldn't come to that. Lt. Wells went on to give his views on the war, boring him to no end with his bravado, until finally they reached the road that led to Bill's plantation.

Bubba and Richard decided to head for the slave quarters to seek out their crew leaders and Meatball; a plan had to be formulated for unloading the wagons and getting those tents set up in a well-organized manner. They found most of the men at the barn. However, this time there was an absence of homebrew and laughter. The men knew that today they would have to make a decision concerning the militia, so naturally that was the topic of conversation; they both just stood there and listened for a while. Bubba finally spoke up and said, "Listen men, Master Bill and I have given you all the reasons why we feel that you should join the militia, and as we've already said, each man should think it over carefully, then follow his heart in making his final decision. Remember, we'll all meet here tonight after supper when we will be signing up the volunteers; keep in mind that some of you will be turned down for military duty, but we will surely need your help in other areas that are just as important to the operation of the unit. It goes without saying that some of us will be wounded or killed, and it really would be nice to have a friend to care for you when that time comes, so please consider that before making your choice." Richard asked Meatball to meet them at the big house with his crew leaders as soon as the meeting ended.

When Meatball finally arrived with his crew leaders they discussed different ways of handling the project and eventually came up with a plan that they all agreed would work. The men suddenly grew very quiet and were looking at one another strangely. Richard asked, "Is something bothering you all?" Sammy was thinking, "Lord, I don't knows why I lets them boys put me up to do the talkin, I show hopes Master Richard don't git mad wid me." His voice shaking as he said, "Well, Master Richard, they show is. You see, the other men and me was talkin after ya'll left and we all figured seein as how most of us grew up together and done suffered through hard times and sickness together, that we want to fight, and if the Lord wills it, die together; it's just simple like that." "So, what are you saying Sammy?" "Beggin your pardon suh, but what I'm sayin is that, if you don't take all of us, you ain't gone git none of us." Richard looked at Sammy in disbelief, and turned to Bubba who was surprised but at the same time understood what Sammy had said. However, this was something he and Bill had not counted on. "But Sammy," said Bubba, "you know that some of these men are hot heads and drink too much and that includes my own brothers; they won't be able to handle the discipline required in military life." "Bubba, you been knowin me all yo life, you know I'm a man of my word and I give you my word that wees gone git these men in shape and I promise that you won't be sorry further down the road." Bubba replied, "I would appreciate it if you men would wait outside while Master Richard and I talk about this; we'll give you our decision shortly." As the men filed out, Richard turned to Bubba. "What are we going to do, Bubba? Do you really think that the men are capable of keeping the hotheads among them in line?" "Richard, I think that people can change if they really want to, and apparently these men do. I also think the spark that will ignite the change in them will be the fear of not measuring up as a man in the eyes of the other men. Anyway, don't I have proof that people can change standing right in front of me? It was just a few days ago that you referred to these men as slaves and black bastards, and just in case you haven't noticed, you now refer to them as men and call them by their names. You, yourself, Richard, have reinforced my belief that people can change and I thank you for that. I only wish Bill were here to give his input on this matter." Richard gave him a queer look. "That wasn't a slip of the tongue, Richard, he and I are on a first name basis also; you see not only is he my Master he's my best friend." "Bubba, they want an answer now, and you know as well as I do that they've got our backs to the wall, so we have no choice but to give in to their demand." Bubba thought for a moment before saying, "Well, knowing Bill as I do, he would feel the same way. However, we're not going to give in to them because they demand it, we're going to give in to them because it's the right thing to do. Do you agree?" " I can't say I don't have some reservations, but I'm beginning to see why they have such respect for you. Lets go tell them."

The men were both relieved and pleased at Bubba and Richard's decision. However, they all agreed that this would affect only the younger men; the older ones would be given supporting roles in the militia. As the four men started to leave, David turned around and said, "Bubba, I can't believe you outright called me a drunk." Bubba put his arm around his brother's shoulder, saying, "Everyone already knows that you're a drunk, David, including you, but I have faith in you to shape up and do the job." David smiled and nodded, continuing on his way.

The plantation was coming into sight; Bill could hardly wait to see Bubba and tell him of the events that took place in Folsom. Yes, he thought, Bubba would be more than glad to see him too, because the atmosphere around here was probably pretty tense since the arrival of Lt. Roach. He stopped the wagon in front of the barn and was immediately surrounded by nearly everyone on the plantation. They had seen him coming and gathered to welcome him back home; they were quite impressed with his uniform. Lt. Wells dismounted from his horse and immediately started doing his impersonation of Napoleon, strutting around, looking at the slaves as if they were his subjects. After assuring himself that the slaves were properly impressed, he turned to Bill and said, "With your permission, Captain, I'll remain here with the men. I'd like a chance to look around this beautiful place you have here, and also take a good look at your slaves." Bill felt a sudden rush of relief. He desperately needed to put some distance between himself and Lt. Wells. As pleasantly as possible, he replied, "As you wish, Lieutenant." As Bill jumped down from the wagon, he thanked them for their show of affection for him and headed straight for his home. When he entered the living room he heard voices coming from the study. Upon investigation, he found Bubba and the Army Officer, Lt. Roach, sitting there talking and laughing as if they were old friends. The sight of the two of them put him at a complete loss for words; he just stood there with what he was sure was an idiotic look on his face.

When Bubba noticed that Bill had returned, he jumped up and greeted him like a long lost brother. It was obvious that he had missed his friend very much. "It really is good to be home Bubba, because the stress of those few days in Folsom made it seem like a month." "Stand back Bill, and let me take a good look at you in that uniform." Bubba smiled and said, "Well, at least it makes you look as if you know what you're doing, even if you don't." "Funny you should say that, Bubba, because the men will more than likely be saying the same thing when you put on the uniform that my tailor made for you." While Bill and Bubba were deeply engaged in conversation, Richard seized the moment and took a good look at this man he had heard so much about. Bill's physique was quite admirable, and at six-foot-two, he towered over Richard and had a manner that inspired respect. Blond, curly hair reaching just to his shoulders, showed off his deeply tanned face to advantage. Obviously an outdoorsman, fine lines were etched around his cobalt blue eyes accustomed to squinting in bright sunlight. He could easily envy the man the attention his rugged good looks would draw from the ladies. But Richard was astute enough to believe that men, too, would show Bill deference and cultivate his friendship. That was certainly apparent in the comfortable and confident way he and Bubba treated one another. Richard cleared his throat to get their attention. Bubba suddenly realized he had forgotten that Richard was even in the room; he apologized for his rudeness and introduced him to Bill. "It's indeed a pleasure to meet you, Lieutenant. I've heard quite a bit about you from your counterpart, Lieutenant Wells, who assured me that you were a very capable officer. I trust that Bubba has taken adequate care of you in my absence?" "Yes Sir, more than adequate. I consider myself a fortunate man to be in his company. Now, if you will excuse me Captain, we've made plans for the unloading of the wagons and we certainly have to get those tents set up before sundown. With your permission, I'll get the men started and return when we're ready to leave for the camp, giving Bubba enough time to fill you in on the progress we've made during your absence. And by the way Captain, do I have your permission to have Lt. Wells assist me?" "You not only have my permission Lt. Roach, you have my blessing," Bill said, throwing a look at Bubba, who got the message.

Bill walked over to the cabinet, pulled out a bottle of brandy, poured himself a drink and said, "Now, my friend, suppose you tell me what the hell is going on? I could not believe my eyes when I walked into this room. From what I was told about this officer, I expected to find you two at each other's throats!" Bubba rubbed his hands together, telling Bill everything that had happened over the past few days, and of the important decision he and Richard had made this very morning, after the men made their terms known. "I think both of you made a wise decision; I don't see how you could have done otherwise." Bill just looked at Bubba speechless for a moment. "Let me make sure I have this straight. You beat Meatball's ass, got the support of all the men, got permission from Miss Martha to court Hattie, converted a bigot, and still managed to complete your project on time. Is that right?" "That's about the gist of it, Bill," Bubba said, with a pleased shrug, as if to say, "Wasn't nothing, Master!" "Well, you've got to be tired as hell, my friend, so get some sleep because when you wake up, I want you to part the Red Sea for me." Once more laughter filled the room that they loved so well. They clasped hands, enjoyed a good laugh together, then turned their attention to the serious concerns awaiting them.

Bill frowned, saying "Bubba, I'm afraid that we are going to have a real problem on our hands with this Lt. Wells. Headquarters assigned him to me as my aide, and there is nothing I can do about it. We are simply stuck with him and I don't think your magic will work on this one; he's a diehard bigot. And the Major is not much better, but thank God, he's being re-assigned to General Lee's outfit." Bill went on to give Bubba all the news of the war, some hard facts and some inevitable rumors. After explaining the plan that headquarters had come up with he said, "I'm hungry. Let's get some breakfast and then you can get into the uniform I brought for you. I need to have a meeting with all the officers before we go to the camp, and you need to be fully, officially dressed. From this point on, we'll have to use our military titles when referring to one another in public. Is that clear, Lieutenant?" "Yes Sir, it certainly is, Captain," Bubba answered smartly, leaving to follow his Captain's first orders.

Bubba, wearing his new Confederate soldier's uniform, stood at attention in front of his mirror, appraising himself. He examined his reflection from every possible angle, his light brown eyes sparkling with good humor. Assuming various poses, he laughed at himself thinking, I'm acting like a silly child! Yet, in spite of his light-hearted manner, he felt a genuine rush of pride in how he looked. Bill's tailor had certainly done excellent work; the uniform flattered his solid, six-foot frame and broad shoulders to perfection. The light-skinned, smooth face gazing at him, seemed to question his youth, as he considered acquiring a manly beard or handsome mustache to make himself appear older and more mature. But that decision could wait. Bubba quickly combed his thick, dark brown hair into place. After one last satisfied glance, he rushed from the room, wondering if his playful antics had made him late for the meeting with Bill and the other officers.

Within the hour, Bubba returned to Bill's study, and found Bill standing by his desk. To Bubba's surprise, Lieutenants Wells and Roach had not yet arrived. Bill looked Bubba up and down and finally said, "I must admit that you look superb Bubba! Hattie will have a tough time fighting the ladies off when they see you in that uniform. I kept my promise to you, persuading the Major into making you my aide in charge of the black soldiers, just as you and I had discussed. But to be honest with you, I had to paint a picture of you being a spy among them, and I must have painted a pretty good one because he readily agreed. However, the next day he informed me that his superiors decided that a slave could not join the Army as an officer, so they offered a compromise of letting you join as a freed slave, but still putting limits on your authority. The idea of a freed slave fighting for the South as an officer, was just too tempting for them to pass up. I did and said anything I had to in order to get what we wanted. A man doesn't always know what he needs in this world, so I count myself lucky to know that I need you standing by my side at any price." Bill reached into his jacket pocket and pulled out a neatly folded paper. "This paper gives you your freedom. Its hard for me to find the words to tell you how proud I am, and what an honor it is to give you my family name, Lt. Shields." No longer able to control his emotions, Bill, with a look of pride in his watery eyes, said, " You'll never know the joy I feel in my heart at this moment, not only for you, but for myself as well. Setting you free, has also freed me of the guilt of having kept you in bondage, and I can only hope that you can forgive me for not having done it sooner." With a shaking hand, Bill slowly handed Bubba the paper. Bubba was so emotionally touched by Bill's words and actions that he was struck dumb. He just kept staring at the document, tears in his eyes, hands beginning to tremble, as he reached out for it. After reading the document, Bubba looked at Bill, his heart pounding! He felt lightheaded, as if he were going to faint. Bubba quickly sat down in his favorite chair. "Are you alright Bubba?" Taking a moment to compose himself, Bubba answered, "Yes, Bill, I guess you could say the shock of this news literally knocked me off my feet! I want you to know that no slave could have asked for a finer Master. Everything you've ever done for me, was done out of love. There is nothing to forgive! I can now stand by your side as a free man, and openly do my part to help our dreams become a reality." Before Bill could respond, Lieutenants Wells and Roach walked in and immediately starting apologizing for being late. Lt. Wells stopped in mid-sentence when he saw Bubba, and looked like he was about to have a stroke. Bill had purposely failed to tell him about Bubba, and the Lieutenant never mentioned it during the trip, so evidently it had also slipped the Major's mind to inform him. "Lt. Wells, seeing that you already know Lt. Roach, let me introduce you to Lt. Shields. He will be in charge of the black troops, act as my aide in that capacity, and report directly to me. As my senior officer and general aide, your duty will be to help coordinate the efforts of both Lt. Shields and Lt. Roach to get these men trained and ready for battle in record time."

Lt. Wells, looking as white as a sheet and totally flabbergasted at what he had just been told said, "With all due respect Sir, are you telling me that I am to be working and consulting with a slave?" "No, I am not, Lieutenant. Lt. Shields is a free man, not a slave, and he will be treated with the respect due any commissioned officer in this Army. You will also notice I have given him my last name, which should tell you how much I value and respect this man. Do I make myself clear?" "Indeed you do, Sir, but I assure you that I will report and protest this matter to the highest authority at headquarters." "In that case Lieutenant, you'll probably be protesting yourself right into a court martial because headquarters gave him his commission. And since we're on this subject, no man in this unit is to be referred to as a slave or any other derogatory names that I'm positive you'd like to use at this very moment." Without giving Lt. Wells a chance to reply he said, " Now that we all understand each other gentlemen, let's get on with the business at hand. I'm anxious to take a look at the work you men have done at the campsite. Lt. Shields, have you assigned a man to stay behind and lead the other men who are coming to join us out to the camp?" "Yes, Sir." Bill rose and walked purposefully out the door saying, "In that case, let's get started."

Lt. Wells was noticeably shaken and seething with anger, but to his credit he managed to contain it, saying "Lt. Roach, I'll be riding in the wagon with you, giving me time to bring you up to date on the current events in Folsom." Richard knew that this man would be seeking him as an ally against Captain Shields, and there was justification for his line of thinking; it was only a few days ago that they held the same views as to how slaves should be treated. There were several wagons lined up at the barn, the others had already left under the supervision of Meatball, who was to get the men started on pitching the tents. Every minute had to be used wisely.

Bill was glad to have the chance to be alone once again with Bubba. There was so much he needed to tell him and this short trip to the camp would give him the opportunity to do that. They had hardly started out when Bubba said, "Bill, you've never had to prove your friendship but if I ever needed proof, today was it. You know this document gives me the right to leave here at any time, so you best stay on my good side." From the look on Bill's face, Bubba could tell that he didn't seem to think that was very funny, which made Bubba laugh all the harder. "Stop looking so serious, Bill, you know I was just kidding! You know I am so grateful for what you've done for me, and thank you for the respect that you are demanding for me from the men. I am sure you're aware of the fact that the actions you've taken have made a sworn enemy of Lt. Wells; he will need to be watched closely." "Yes, I'm afraid you're right, Bubba. I don't think he'll be able to control his rage for long; he's probably planning some way to circumvent my authority as we speak, and no doubt attempting to enlist the aid of Lt. Roach to become his accomplice.

A devious mind such as his will try to spread its poison to the white soldiers in the unit. Then we'll really have problems. We are going to have to find a way to deal with him before he causes us serious harm." Tired of addressing problems, Bill decided to confide in Bubba and told him about the conversation he and Mona had concerning the possibility of marriage when the war was over. After giving Bill's situation some thought Bubba said, "If she truly loves you, Bill, and you have the same feelings for her, to hell with what people may think, you should be with the woman that makes you happy; maybe we could have a double wedding."

While Bill and Bubba were engaged in their private conversation, Lt. Wells didn't waste any time. He started right in on Richard, expecting to make him an ally by saying, "The Major was absolutely right about that slave-loving bastard. If he thinks that I'm going to stand still for this, he's sadly mistaken. The idea of us treating slaves like they are our equals is preposterous. I don't know why in God's name the Major gave that black monkey a commission, but I do know that something is not quite right here, and I intend to get to the bottom of it. When all the white soldiers arrive we'll inform them of the situation, and I'm sure that they will agree that the Captain and that monkey in an officer's uniform will have to be disposed of. Once we've taken care of them, as senior officer, I will assume command of the unit and get these slaves and poor white trash trained so they can die when our plan calls for it." Richard looked at Lt. Wells and hated what he saw, because it was a mirror image of himself just a short time ago, and he felt ashamed. How could he have been so insensitive to the needs and feelings of those who were in bondage? He could use his upbringing as an excuse, but somehow that thought did not give him comfort because he now knew that there is no excuse for such behavior. He vowed to himself never to return to being the man he had been - like the man now looking at him for his support. Being a realist, Richard realized that for now he would have to play along with Lt. Wells, better to be on the inside seen as a friend, than on the outside as an enemy; in this way he would be in a position to foil any attempt on the life of the Captain or Bubba. He replied, "I'm inclined to agree with you, Lieutenant. We can discuss this matter further when the day's work is done, but don't tell the other men just yet. I think I can come up with a much better plan that will put an end to this problem. A room has been prepared for you in the main house until our quarters have been made ready. We'll meet in the barn tonight after everyone is asleep, which should be around ten o'clock."

As Lt. Wells left him, Lt. Roach thought, I'm sincerely pleased with the friendship Bubba and I have established. Though I only met the Captain briefly, my instincts tell me he is a man I could totally respect; they both seem to be honorable men. I cannot possibly allow this crazed man to carry out an act of vengeance against them. Richard knew at some point he must tell Bubba and the Captain, of the secret alternate plan headquarters had, but first he must deal with the current problem, Lt. Wells.

When they drove into the camp the sight of several tents already in place impressed them; Meatball was doing an excellent job at supervising the men. Sammy was putting his building skills to work, shouting out to enlist his men where help was needed. When Bubba got out of the wagon the men shouted and cheered, seeing him for the first time in uniform; the look in their eyes told him how proud they were of him.

Bill and his lieutenants went on a tour of the camp. It was hard to believe that all this was accomplished in a matter of days; he congratulated Bubba and Richard again on their outstanding work, while Lt. Wells remained silent during the whole tour. He kept looking at Bill and Bubba as if his mind were cooking up some evil deed. Bill shouted out to the men, "You men have done a fine job here, but there is much more to be done; we must have these tents ready for the men who are arriving, before sundown. Can we do it?" They all shouted back, "Yes, Sir!" Bill looked at all the attentive faces and said, "I have been informed of your desire to sign up for the militia without any able bodied man being rejected, and the work that you've done here proves to me that you can work together without problems and get the job done. I am in full agreement with the decision that was made. You will be listed as members of the unit when you enter the camp tomorrow. Don't forget, you men need to say your goodbyes to your families tonight because you all will be quartered here for the duration of the war; but you will be allowed to visit them at the end of your training period. And so there is no confusion, I'm honored to say Bubba has agreed to take my surname, Shields; it sounds a lot better than Lt. Bubba." The men shouted their approval with good-natured laughter and went back to work. They worked late into the evening, and as luck would have it, just as they were putting up the last tent someone spotted the wagon train of volunteers coming in the distance. Thanks to Sammy and Arthur, the cooking tents were set up earlier, with pots brimming with hot stew and coffee to feed the men; all of the essentials to begin training were in place.

Sergeant Kimbro had the men unload the wagons. Bill was impressed by the Sergeant's control of his men; they quickly responded to his every command. Standing about six feet tall, even at the age of thirty-eight his lean body looked as hard as steel. His men could tell if they were performing their duties properly just by looking into his cold gray eyes. As he ran his hand through his long sandy hair, and wiped the sweat (caused by the morning heat) from his smooth and darkly tanned face, he shouted, "You there! Soldier! Be careful with that crate!" When that task was finished, Sergeant Kimbro had the men line up for inspection. Bill was somewhat disappointed at the number of men that were present; the Sergeant explained that some of them had changed their minds at the last moment. Bill nodded and said, "Maybe it's for the best, better to weed out the ones now who have no stomach for fighting than have them desert later." Bill addressed the men, thanking them for volunteering and assuring them that they would be treated with the same respect as any other soldier in the Confederate Army. "Lt. Shields will show you where these men and the regular soldiers are to be quartered, Sergeant Kimbro." "Yes, Sir." The Sergeant, shocked into silence, stared at Bubba as he led the men to their quarters. After making sure that the new men were properly taken care of, and necessary daily living assignments were given to a few selected men, they began the trip back home.

Lt. Wells was completely silent on the return trip. When they reached the big house he leaned over to Richard and whispered, "Don't forget, tonight at ten o'clock", and then asked to be shown directly to his room where he would remain until his meeting with Richard later on in the barn. He felt somewhat reassured by the thought that Lt. Roach had a plan to help put an end to what he saw as insanity on the part of Captain Shields.

Bill, Bubba and Richard retired to the study after supper to discuss the progress they had made that day. Bill said, "The men can finish up where needed after they report to the camp tomorrow. Sunday can be spent resting and becoming accustomed to their new surroundings, so they'll be ready to start training on Monday morning." After all the business was handled, Bubba asked to be excused in order to spend some time with his parents and Hattie. He, as well as the other men, had never been away from their families for even a short period of time, let alone four weeks; it would take some getting used to. Richard, looking concerned said, "Before you leave, Bubba, I'd like to bring up the subject of Lt. Wells. In my personal opinion, Lt. Wells has allowed his bigoted attitude to push him over the edge. His complete silence during the tour of the camp, and on the trip back here, indicates a person about to suffer a nervous breakdown; even his own men noticed his strange behavior." "Yes, Lt. Roach, I, too, feel that there is a serious problem in the making. What's your opinion, Lt. Shields?" " Captain, the look I saw in that man's eyes today was one of pure evil. I totally agree with Lt. Roach, we've got a serious situation to deal with." "Well, gentlemen," said Bill, "it seems my concerns about Lt. Wells are well founded. His stubborn resistance to change could bring tremendous harm to the unit, and possibly undo everything we've worked for. I suggest we keep a careful watch on him, perhaps this way we can possibly stop him from carrying out any mischief he may be planning. In the meantime, Let's hope that after a few hours of rest, he'll be rational enough to listen to our plans for this militia unit. He might even reconsider his views once he's heard us out. I realize that I'm putting hope against hope, but I am sure you both will agree that we have to give him a chance; do we have an understanding, gentlemen?" Bubba and Richard halfheartedly replied, "Yes, Sir." "Well, in that case, I'll say goodnight; there is much to be done in the morning."

Bill remained seated at the desk pondering the conversation that had just taken place. His instincts told him that Lt. Roach knew much more about what Lt. Wells was planning than he was willing to say, and he'd be willing to bet that it had something to do with harming Bubba. Bill decided to put the matter aside for the moment and get some sleep. Tomorrow would be a trying day.

Bubba, with Hattie by his side, sat around the kitchen table with his family laughing, and as always, telling jokes. David and Jab asked when they were going to get their uniforms so they could have women runnin after them, too. Louie said, "The last time women were runnin after you two they had knives in they hands." No one escaped their turn to be made the butt of good-natured fun; they knew that this would probably be the last time they would be together as a family before the horror of war would take its toll.

It was dark and quiet on the plantation, which made it much easier for Richard to make his way to the barn without being seen. He had stopped to alert Lt. Wells before leaving the house, but found his room empty, and reeking of whiskey. Richard thought, apparently Lt. Wells is fortifying himself with enough courage to carry out his own sinister plan, if he decides he can't rely on me to become his accomplice to murder. Richard wasn't sure of what his intentions were concerning Lt. Wells, but he was prepared to go to any lengths to stop this idiot from killing Bubba and Captain Shields.

Richard entered the barn, and there stood Lt. Wells, with a bottle of whiskey in one hand, pacing back and forth, mumbling to himself. Richard announced his presence by saying, "Lt. Wells, I think you've had a bit too much to drink, perhaps we had better have our discussion when you are sober enough to realize the consequences of your intended actions toward Lt. Shields and the Captain." At the sound of Richard's voice, Lt. Wells stopped pacing, turned and looked at Richard, and with an obvious slur, said "Just tell me one thing, Lt. Roach. Have you come up with a workable plan?" "First, Lieutenant, I need to ask you if you're absolutely sure you want to go through with this?" Lt. Wells, eyes burning, answered, "There is nothing I want more than to see both of those bastards dead! It's the only way to put an end to this equality bullshit." Lt. Roach felt chilled to the bone and flushed with heat at hearing those hate-filled words. "Is there nothing else you can think of, short of killing them?" Lt. Wells snarled, "Nothing that would give me as much satisfaction! I'm asking again, Lt. Roach, have you come up with a plan to put an end to this madness?" With a voice filled with determination, Lt. Roach replied, "Yes, Lt. Wells, I certainly have. I've decided that I cannot allow you to murder two of the most admirable men it's ever been my pleasure to meet. You leave me no choice, but to expose your treacherous intentions to the Captain." Enraged, Lt. Wells yelled out, "Why you back-stabbing son-of-a-bitch!" While uttering those nasty words, he staggered toward Lt. Roach, pulling a concealed revolver from his waistband.

The black night, wrapped in peaceful starlight only moments before, was brutally punctured by a gunshot. Bill, sleeping fitfully, was quickly aroused out of a bad dream. He shook himself awake and heard only silence. But, Bill knew that sound; he reached for his trousers and pulled them on as he ran from the house. He had no way of knowing where the shot came from, so he stood there, eyes adjusting to the darkness, until he saw men running toward the barn shouting, "The shot came from there!" With a sense of deep foreboding, he started running in that direction.

Lt. Roach was standing in the doorway of the barn, hands soaked with blood. The look on Richard's face told Bill of the horror that waited to be discovered. "Lt. Roach, what in the hell is going on here? I thought I heard a gunshot, and by the blood on your hands, I can see I was not mistaken." Lt. Roach, looking at his blood-splattered hands, slowly answered, "It's Lt. Wells, Sir, he's inside." Bill rushed into the barn and found Lt. Wells lying on the ground, his chest seeping blood. It seemed that even in death, his cold, vacant eyes still had a look of evil about them. The other men began to enter the barn, each man visibly shaken at the sight of Lt. Wells lying there, dead. Bill detected the distinct odor of whiskey, as he examined the lifeless body, and discovered that Lt. Wells had been shot in the heart. Bubba, pushing his way through the crowd of men, was stunned by the scene. "Oh, my God! Captain! What happened here?" "All I know for sure Lt. Shields, is that this man has been shot through the heart, but you can bet I'm going to get to the bottom of it, before this night is over! Some of you men, cover this poor fellow's body, there is nothing we can do for him; he's now in God's hands. I know that you are upset by this terrible event, but we must carry on. I am sure that this will be a restless night for you, but I'm asking that you return to your homes and spend the precious time you have left with your families." The men slowly starting drifting towards home, each of them lost in his own thoughts. "Lt. Roach, report to my office, at once! Lt. Shields, you go along to bear witness to any statements Lt. Roach cares to make, concerning this incident."

Richard who had been strangely silent the whole time, decided he would tell the Captain the truth about Lt. Wells' plan to murder him and Bubba, allowing him to assume command of the militia unit. He would also tell the Captain of the part he played, with the intention of foiling the scheme. Richard's conscience was tugging at him to also tell the Captain about the alternate plan headquarters had for their unit. But hadn't there been enough horror and tragedy for one night? He needed to be told, and he would tell him when the time was right. It might even be possible that a new order would come from headquarters, and he would have caused a stir for nothing. Richard's mind was full of turmoil as he struggled with this dilemma.

As Bubba and Richard solemnly walked to the big house, Richard said, "Bubba, I know how this looks, but I swear to you, I did not kill him. That's not to say that I did not entertain the thought, but when it came down to it, I just couldn't bring myself to do it. Bubba, you must believe me! I swear to you! I did not kill Lt. Wells!" "Don't worry Richard. We've only known each other for a short time, but I know enough about you to say I'm positive that the death of Lt. Wells was caused by an act of self-defense or a tragic accident. I'm sure that once you tell Bill what occurred in that barn, he'll come to the same conclusion."

Bill purposely stayed behind after everyone had left. He suddenly remembered that Lt. Roach had no revolver in his hand, or from what he could see, on his person, when Bill arrived at the barn. Bill picked up a lantern, and began searching the barn. He spotted a gun near Lt. Well's lifeless body, the blanket now covering him stained with rivers of his blood. Kneeling down, after close examination, Bill knew that the revolver had been recently fired; the smell of gunpowder was strong in the barrel, evidenced by an empty shell casing, still in the chamber. What possibly could have transpired between Lt.

Roach and this man that would cost him his life? With gun in hand, Bill left the barn, praying Lt. Roach had answers that would exonerate him of any wrongdoing.

When Bill entered his study (which also served as his temporary office), he found Bubba and Richard engaged in what appeared to be an emotional conversation. They ceased talking, and started to rise as Bill entered the room. Bill did not waste any time, "Remain seated gentlemen, and tonight I don't have time for this formal military bullshit! Richard, I believe you to be an honorable man, therefore I expect you to tell us the truth about what occurred in that barn tonight, and why you and Lt. Wells felt it necessary to sneak out of the house in the middle of the night, to meet there in the first place!" Before Richard could answer Bill's question, Bubba spoke out, "Bill! Surely you don't believe that the death of Lt. Wells was anything other than an accident?" "Of course not, Bubba, but I doubt if headquarters will see it that way, without a detailed description of what actually took place to cause his death. Now, Richard, would you calmly tell us what happened and why?"

Richard was relieved to know Bill was willing to consider giving him the benefit of the doubt. After standing up, Richard began telling Bill and Bubba everything that led up to the planned rendezvous at the barn. After clearing his throat, he continued, "When I entered the barn, I found Lt. Wells pacing back and forth, ranting and raving incoherently. Believe me, I tried to reason with him, but the whiskey he had consumed and his obvious rage, had gotten the better of him; he refused to consider anything short of murdering you and Bubba. I decided that a continued attempt at reasoning with him would be futile. When I informed him that I was going to report his treacherous intentions to you, he came at me like a mad dog! While pulling his revolver and rushing toward me, the Lieutenant tripped, accidentally shooting himself. Although he was not deserving of it, I ran to his aid, but blood was spurting everywhere. I realized the bullet had entered his heart, killing him instantly. I only have God as my witness, but I swear on everything that is sacred to me; I have told you the absolute, horrible truth."

Richard looked at Bill, his eyes pleading for understanding. " Before I make any comment on your explanation, Richard, I must ask you to show me your revolver. It is in your possession, isn't it?" "Yes, Bill, it is. I tucked it away in my waistband, and pulled my shirt over it, to avoid it being detected. I can't stand here and tell you that I wouldn't have used it in self-defense, but I never got a chance to make that decision." "In that case, Richard, you won't mind if I take a look at your revolver, will you?" Richard did not answer Bill. He simply raised his shirt, removed his revolver from his waistband, and handed it to him. While reaching out to take the weapon, Bill thought, Lord, please let me be right in my belief that this man is innocent. Bubba had quickly caught on to Bill's intention and waited for his assessment. Although Richard knew he was innocent, fear began to overtake him as he watched Bill expertly examine the revolver. He, too, understood the purpose, and that his life hung in the balance. Bill, giving a sigh of relief, said, "It seems, Richard, in my opinion, you are telling the truth; your weapon has not been fired recently. After everyone left the barn, I examined the body of Lt. Wells and his revolver. What I found, coupled with the strong odor of whiskey about him, corroborates your story. I must tell you that I'm very pleased at this outcome, as I am sure you are. But I'm also quite saddened that men such as Lt. Wells can be filled with so much hate, that it blinds them to the fact that no man can be free, until all men are free." Richard, who was quite relieved by Bill's decision, but still evidently shaken by tonight's events said, "Bill, I would like to thank you for taking the time to thoroughly investigate the situation before judging my guilt or innocence. I doubt if another commander put in that position, would have bothered to take the time. You, Sir, are an honorable man, and it is my honor, to serve under your command." Richard then turned to Bubba, "Not knowing my innocence or guilt, you still chose to stand by me, and for that act of loyalty you have my undying gratitude." Bubba replied, "I once read that if you believe in good, you must also believe in evil, because one cannot exist without the other; let's just be thankful that God chose to remove what was evil in our lives, and left the good."

"Well, Gentlemen", said Bill, "Now that this whole unfortunate incident has been cleared up, I suppose we must return to military formality. It goes without saying, Lt. Roach that Bubba and I are in your debt, and we possibly owe our very lives to you. God knows what might have happened if you had not intervened, but my guess is, we probably would have been murdered in our sleep." Bubba, with a look of concern on his face said, "We must stay alert, should another Lt. Wells be lurking among us. To be completely honest with both of you, I can't find it in my heart to feel any pity for Lt. Wells. Now my only hope is that there is no such thing as reincarnation; just the thought of a bastard like that returning to earth in any form scares the hell out of me." Bill, standing to stretch his tired body, replied, "That indeed, is a terrifying thought."

In the morning, Lt. Shields, please have someone ride to the camp and have the Sergeant bring a small detachment of men here. I'll inform him of the situation when he arrives. We'll assign a man to escort the body of Lt. Wells home. I'll write a letter to his family explaining the tragic accident that led to his death; naturally I'll leave out the dishonorable details. No words could ever erase the pain of losing their son, but at least they'll have the comfort of knowing he died quickly, the result of an accident, with no mention of his drunkenness. A messenger will be sent to headquarters in the morning informing them of his death and the circumstances surrounding it. They'll also be informed that Lt. Roach is quite capable of carrying on, so there will be no need to send a replacement. We'll give an appropriate farewell to Lt. Wells in the morning and move on. Right now, we had better take advantage of what's left of the night and try to get some rest." Bubba could feel his friend's exhaustion. Sighing deeply, Bill said, "But before I do, I need to write those letters; so I'll say goodnight to you gentlemen." Bubba, placed his hand on Richard's shoulder, saying quietly, "Get some rest, my friend. Lt. Wells fell victim to his own bigotry, and that's the truth." Bubba left the room, convinced that justice had been served. Richard headed toward his room, anticipating a troubled, sleepless night.

The morning came too quickly for Bill. After discovering that Lt. Roach had already left, he ate a hurried breakfast, then headed for the barn where he found Bubba and Richard waiting. The Sergeant and his men arrived just a few minutes later. The Sergeant smartly marched up to Bill saying, "Sergeant Kimbro, reporting as ordered, Sir!" Bill replied, "At ease Sergeant." He quickly took him aside and explained in detail what had taken place concerning the death of Lt. Wells. The sergeant looked Bill straight in the eyes and said, "Begging your pardon, Sir, but I never did trust that little beady-eyed bastard." Bill was so shocked by the Sergeant's words that he was utterly speechless. Sgt. Kimbro showed no sign of remorse at hearing of his Lieutenant's death. Bill thought, how strange? This was definitely not the response he had expected from the Sergeant. However, Bill gave no reply to the Sergeant's harsh words. He simply gave him his instructions and dismissed him.

Sgt. Kimbro and his men were instructed to put the body of Lt. Wells, which lay in a wooden coffin that Sammy had hastily constructed, onto the wagon. He called all the men together and they paid their last respects to a man they hardly knew. Bill gave the family's letter to the driver to deliver, and then asked to see the soldier who had been chosen to deliver the message to headquarters. It was now time to start a hard day's work.

CHAPTER FOURTEEN

Bill turned to Bubba. "Lt. Shields, are the men ready to start the move to the camp?" "Yes, Sir. I told them that they could have a few more minutes to spend with their loved ones." "Good idea, Lieutenant. Take some time and do the same," Bill said, lost in his own thoughts, as Bubba saluted with a quick, "Thank you, Sir."

Bubba rushed home to say his final goodbyes to his mother and sister, knowing Hattie would come over to spend what little time they had left, together. When he entered the cabin he found not only his brothers packed and ready to leave, but also his father. Bubba smiled, hands on his hips, "Daddy, just where do you think you're going?" Louie gazed up at his son, saying, "Your mama and me have done talked it over son. I been lookin after you boys all yo lives and I ain't gone stop now. I may not be able to keep up with you boys when it come to doin all that fancy trainin and such, but I'm still a good man

176

to have round," Louie said proudly. "I aims to do my part to help you whip them Yankees and anybody else that tries to bring harm to ya'll. Bubba, you know just as well as I do that they is still some peckerwoods in that camp that won't take kindly to a black man that even look like he in charge of somethin, let lone in charge of somethin. I be there watchin out for you cause even with all that book learnin, you still needs these old eyes in the back a my head, I'm tellin ya." Bubba looked surprised, hearing these words. "Daddy, what are you talking about?" "You know damn well what I'm talkin bout. I may be old but I ain't no old fool. The man layin in that coffin out there was put down by the Lord, like the mad dog he was. Us black folks knows evil when we sees it, and that man was pure evil. This might not be real Christian, but I hope God give his kind a special place in hell. Now lets git on outa here befoe these women start up cryin, agin."

The wagons were loaded with the needed supplies along with the men's personal belongings. All goodbyes had been said, some tearfully but most of them encouraging as well; they were ready to meet whatever lay ahead.

When they entered the camp it seemed that the men from the other plantations and soldiers had settled in pretty good; they looked at ease in their new surroundings. Bill instructed the sergeant to see that the men were shown to their quarters and then report back to him. Bill went directly to his quarters, taking Bubba and Richard along with him. They had done a fine job of outfitting the tent, even down to a table and chairs. Richard said, "Bubba do you think our quarters (which were located next to Bill's tent), will be as accommodating as this?" "Why, sure Richard, just like I believe that it occasionally rains in hell." Bill smirked at Bubba's joke. "When this war is over, I'll get you both jobs touring the South as a comedy team."

Sgt. Kimbro reported back to Bill, as instructed. "Will there be anything else, Sir?" "Yes, Sergeant, I know it's only been a short time, but how do you feel the men are getting along?" Sgt. Kimbro thought for a moment before responding, "They seem to be getting on really well, Sir. If I may take the liberty of saying so, Captain, all of my men were hand picked by me. Knowing what the situation would be, I chose only men that I knew bore no ill will toward blacks. That's not to say they won't have problems accepting them as equals when it comes to soldiering, but it should be easier for them to make the adjustment." Bill nodded his agreement. "You seem to have everything under control, Sergeant. May I ask why you seem to have such empathy for blacks?" "Well, Sir, seeing as how you gentlemen are fair and understanding men, I'll tell you something that only my family knows about me. Lt. Shields, when I saw you yesterday, I was completely caught off guard at seeing a black man in the uniform of a Confederate Officer. The look on my face was one of complete surprise, not disgust." The Sergeant cleared his throat and went on. "As a young girl, my mother fell in love with a man who sometimes worked around our place as a handyman, and they ended up having an affair. When her father found out about it, he became so outraged that he shot and killed the man. He later found out that she was pregnant, and sent her to Alabama to stay with relatives to avoid embarrassment. I am the result of that affair, and the man that my grandfather killed was a freed slave. My family passed me off as white, but I was a constant reminder to them of the shame they felt my mother brought on them. As soon as I was old enough, I ran away and joined the army and haven't been back since. I was once married, but army life took its toll on the marriage, and my wife left me and moved to Maryland, along with my daughter, Geraldine; its been years since I've seen them." The sergeant turned away for a minute, getting his emotions under control. "I've been wanting to tell that story to someone for years; I'm asking that you hold what I've said here in strict confidence. I'm just glad I finally met people that I could tell the truth to. Gentlemen, it's because of the compassion that I see in you that gave me the courage to tell you my story." And with that said,

Sgt. Kimbro saluted them, turned around, and began to walk away. Bubba touched his arm, saying, "Sergeant, may I ask what became of your mother?" Sgt. Kimbro stopped, a deep sadness in his voice. "She died still grieving the death of my father when I was still a young boy. Now if you'll excuse me, Sir, I need to check on the men." Bill, lost for words after hearing the Sergeant's story, finally turned his attention back to his Lieutenants saying, "Gentlemen, I think that's one of the saddest stories I've ever heard, but I'm grateful that Sgt. Kimbro felt he could share it with us without putting himself at risk. The good news is that now we can get this phase of the project done without constantly looking over our shoulders. Lets get all of the loose ends tied up today. Lt. Roach, do you have a training program set up?" "Yes, Sir, the Sergeant and his men are more than familiar with the standard training procedures and they are to be implemented Monday morning at daybreak." Bill turned his attention on Bubba. "Lt. Shields, you and I will be taking a crash course in military tactics; with the help of Lt. Roach and the military manuals I brought along, come Monday morning we should be able to lead this unit straight to hell." Bubba said, "Yes, Captain, that's what I'm afraid of!" They all laughed nervously, each man knowing the significance of this training.

Twenty-eight days of intense training had come to an end. The men had done surprisingly well, considering their varied backgrounds. They managed somehow to form a strong bond among them that was essential in a military unit. Although most had become homesick, not one man gave into the temptation to sneak out of camp and head for home. Lt. Roach and the Sergeant had successfully completed the task of training these men far beyond Bill's expectations.

Bill had received word the previous week that the men's uniforms were ready to be picked up in Folsom. The soldier sent to pick them up would be returning within the hour; going home on leave and showing off their new uniforms, would be another proud moment for the men and for him. Not only was Bill excited about the uniforms arriving, he was also anxious to receive the dispatches telling him how the war was progressing, and when he might expect to engage the enemy.

Bubba and Richard spotted the wagon approaching and rushed to inform Bill, who asked them to get the soldiers into formation. The men were ready in record time. Bill walked outside, climbed up on the wagon and said, " Men, first of all, let me tell you how proud I am of you. Your dedication and hard work throughout the training program has earned you the right to wear the uniform of a soldier in the Army of the Confederates States of America. He tossed one of the hats into the air, shouting, "Wear them proudly!" The men went wild in the spirit of the moment, slapping each other on the back, congratulating each other and as always, joking. Louie, who had opted to train with the men who would be serving as medics said, "Lt. Shields, I think maybe you and yo brothers best find ya'll somewheres else to sleep tonight, cause when you mama see me in this uniform ain't no tellin what gonna happen." Arthur yelled out, "Yeah, they show gone be plenty of lovin goin on tonight."

As Richard watched the men, a feeling of guilt began to totally consume him. He decided the time had come to tell Bill that the plans he received for the defense of Folsom had been concocted by the Major and General staff at headquarters in order to hide the real purpose for forming this militia unit. He knew that one of the dispatches (as previously planned), would contain a letter informing him that the Yankees were heading toward Folsom with a small force and that he was to prepare to engage them in battle. The estimated time of their arrival would be given as three days from the receipt of the letter. It would also state that Lt. Roach was to report back to headquarters at the end of his training assignment, as he would be needed there to carry out other duties.

After accepting the dispatches from the driver, Bill said, "Well, soldier, how does Folsom seem to be coping with the war?" "Sir, it was really kind of strange; except for a few officers sitting around in the Major's old office, there didn't seem to be another soldier in sight. When I inquired as to their whereabouts they just handed me the dispatches, told me where the uniforms were stored, then advised me to be on my way. By the time I got the wagon loaded I noticed that they, too, were heading out of town. Begging your pardon, Sir, but I've been wondering how are they going to come to our aid if we don't even know where they are?" Bill paused for what seemed like a long moment. "I can see, soldier, that your mother did not raise a fool; you're dismissed."

"Lt. Roach, I need to see you and Lt. Shields in my quarters immediately." Just as he was about to open the dispatches, Bill looked up at them and said, "Gentlemen, the soldier who delivered these has just confirmed a suspicion that I've been harboring for some time now; the Major has some other kind of agenda in mind for us while keeping us in the dark." He then shared the soldier's comments, and said, "Headquarters was to keep us informed of the whereabouts of the main body of soldiers at all times." Bill looked both angry and perplexed. "It looks as though we've been hung out to dry without any explanation." Richard swallowed and summoned up the courage to say, "But I'm afraid there is an explanation, Sir." With great effort at control, Bill asked coldly, "And just what might that be, Lt. Roach?" Richard withered beneath Bill's stare and quietly spoke, "Sir, I'm ashamed to say that your suspicions are correct; I have firsthand knowledge of a plan that was devised to send you and your soldiers to your deaths, because I was initially involved in that deception." Bill's eyes seemed to smoke as they fastened on Richard, and with a look of total frustration, he said, "Tell us everything you know right now about this and why you waited until now to speak!"

Richard quickly explained how and why the plan was conceived, and that he and Lt. Wells had been ordered to take on the mission of training the militia to ensure that the deception would go smoothly. He told Bill the contents of the letter that he would find in his dispatches. Richard looked at Bubba and said, "What I did not count on was developing a friendship that changed my whole concept of how slaves should be looked upon and treated. I had every intention of telling you earlier, but I just couldn't seem to find the right time to do it. You must believe me when I say that I had made up my mind to tell you this very day. After seeing the look of pride on the faces of the men when they received their uniforms, I knew that I could not keep silent any longer. The fear of you knowing that I had played a part in such a horrible plan kept holding me back from being honest with you. The last thing I want is to lose the respect and trust that you both have given me; I hope you can understand my reluctance to ruin the bonds we have formed, and find it in your hearts to forgive me. I'm a different man now than I was when I agreed to the Major's plan."

Bubba walked over to Richard, put his hands on his shoulders, saying, "You are forgiven. Each man chooses the road he walks down, and I believe that your actions proved that long before this day, you chose to walk with us and not against us. I think Bill will agree that we need to put this matter behind us and move on." Bill offered his hand to Richard, who clasped it tightly, relief visible on his face. "Bubba is absolutely right. What we need now Richard, is a plan of action that will circumvent their plan to betray us." Then Bill opened the dispatch pouch and pulled out the letter; Richard was telling the truth.

The work on a plan to foil the Major began. After much discussion, Lt. Roach spoke up. "Captain, I have an idea that I've been toying with for the past few weeks, but it will take some powerful acting on Bubba's part." Bill interrupted Lt. Roach, "This letter states that you return to headquarters when your training assignment is completed." "Well Sir," he responded firmly, "I guess this will be the first time in my career that I've disobeyed an order." "In that case, Lieutenant, tell us about this scheme of yours." "First of all, Sir, we don't have three days until the Yankees arrive, we only have two. The third day was added so that the Yankees would catch you off guard, and they won't be a small force to contend with because compared to our numbers, it will seem like the whole Union Army. The reason that so many soldiers are converging on us is because false information was leaked to the Yankees that a significant force, totally unprepared for an attack, is located here. Naturally, the North would see this as an opportunity to win a quick victory and possibly weaken the will of the Southern soldiers to fight. I see this as a case of "do unto others as they would have done unto you," only we have to do it much faster." Richard appealed to Bubba for special help. "Bubba, I know that the slaves have a grapevine system that tells them anything they want to know. Can we use it to find out where those soldiers were headed when they left Folsom?" Bubba replied, "That's good thinking, Richard, but what good is that information?" "All the good in the world, if we can put the Yankees on their trail. That's where you come in, Bubba. Once you have that information, you'll travel by wagon with several of our men until you locate the Yankees pretending to be escaped, mistreated slaves. In order to keep from drawing suspicion, you won't give them the information right off. You'll just sort of dangle it in front of them. I have no doubt that they will bite. The idea is to encourage them to split their forces based on your information, using the majority of their men to give chase to those bastards who would have left us here to die. We have to hope that their commanding officer is a glory seeker and won't be able to resist the temptation of giving chase to what he perceives to be a fleeing army. If we can pull this off, the battle will start on our terms; at least we'll have a chance for survival, and not fall victim to the slaughter headquarters had in mind for us."

Bill and Bubba exchanged a look born of years of shared thought and experiences, before Bill said, "Lieutenant, I'm sure glad that you're on our side. It's clear to me that you've given this plan of yours considerable thought. I think it's a bit risky, but the silver tongue of Lt. Shields has amazed me in the past. What do you think, Bubba? Can you do it one more time?" Bubba took a deep breath, squaring his massive shoulders. "Gentlemen, I think that I'm about to give the performance of my life!" Bill stood and shook their hands. "Gentlemen, we have very little time to pull this off, so I suggest we get started right away. Bubba, how soon do you think it will take you to get the information we need?" "Just as soon as I reach Folsom. There's an old man who cleans all the official offices in town, and that includes the Major's office. He's been there so long, they talk around him like he's invisible, but that man knows everything going on in Folsom; whenever we want to know white folks' business, he's the man we see." "Great. Pick the men you'll need for this assignment and get going; we don't have a minute to waste. Once you have what you need, locate the Yankees and put on a show that convinces them to locate our Army." Bill looked solemn, as he put his arm around Bubba's shoulders. "Be very careful my friend; if things go wrong, you'll be at their mercy and that's something I don't even want to think about." "Don't worry, Bill, you know me. I plan on returning safe and sound with my men at my side. We're gonna dangle the bait right in front of their noses. They won't be able to resist taking it!"

Bill silently applauded Bubba's bravado in the face of real danger. Then Bubba turned suddenly serious. "Bill, I think it would be not only wise, but also fair, to tell the men exactly what's going on, and what we plan to do to remedy the situation; they deserve to have a say in this matter." "As always, Bubba, you show good judgment. We'll call the men together now and let them make their choice."

When they had formed up, Bill told them the truth of how and why they had been betrayed. He also explained Lt. Roach's plan in detail, and what he expected to gain from it. "None of you men signed up for a possible suicide mission, but it seems that our backs are against the wall. We are left with no choice, but to connive and fight our way out of this situation. Due to the seriousness of the situation, I'm willing to listen to any of your comments on the plan we've devised." The men stood as one, totally silent. At last, Sergeant Kimbro spoke up, "Captain, Sir, I'm sure I speak for the rest of the men when I say, we'd follow you to hell and back!" The men suddenly broke formation, running toward Bill, cheering! "Well," said Sgt. Kimbro, "it looks like we're all with you, Sir." Bill looked at these men with pride, shouting, "Men, we have a lot to lose if this plan fails, get ready to put it all on the line! If we live through this, one day I'll be able to tell my children that I fought with some of the finest men in the Confederate Army. Slowly, Bill raised his hand in a salute.

"As you know, my intentions were to give you several days to spend with your families, but that's no longer possible because we have so little time to prepare for battle. You have only what remains of today and tonight to be with your loved ones, because at daybreak Lt. Roach and Sgt. Kimbro will be instructing you in the tactics we will use in the coming fight. Lt. Shields should be returning by tomorrow evening when we'll know for sure whether or not our plan to redirect some of the Union soldiers was successful. Lt. Shields will choose several of you men to accompany him. If any of you want to volunteer, report to him. You're dismissed."

Volunteers immediately approached Bubba, but he said, "I appreciate the fact that you men are willing to go with me, but I've already selected the soldiers for this mission. Before this is over, I'm sure that you will have many chances to volunteer for something; after all, this is the Army. Right now, I want Sammy, David, Arthur and Meatball to report to my quarters." As the four men entered his tent, he noticed his father bringing up the rear. Shaking his head, Bubba said, "Daddy, what are you doing here? I didn't call your name." Louie planted himself in front of his son. "There ain't no sense in arguin with me son, cause I'm comin long. Where you go, I go, and you ain't goin nowhere that I can't watch ovah you; now lets git on with this meetin." Bubba shrugged, knowing there was no way to talk him out of it. "Listen up, men. We will take only enough food and water to last us until we get back, and revolvers which we can easily hide in the wagon. Let's pray we won't need them, but it's wise to have them handy. Remember now, when we locate the Yankees we have to appear to be runaway slaves and practically kiss their ass for coming to free us." Louie laughed, saying, "There's one good thang bout this Bubba, I mean Lieutenant; when it come to kissin white folks' asses we don't need no practice. That's why most black folks got big lips.

190

We done puckered up so much just to survive, that they wouldn't go back down." "Daddy, this is no time for your jokes," Bubba said, trying to hide his smile. "That weren't no joke Bubba; it's the damn truth." "Alright, daddy, you've made your point. Now please go with these men and help put the supplies on the wagon. We'll be leaving within the hour because the quicker we can get this done, the quicker we can get back and spend a few hours at home."

With the men gone, Bubba entered Bill's quarters and found him alone. "We'll be ready to leave soon, and I just wanted to say...." Bill held up his hand. "Don't even think about saying it Bubba, because I know you and your men will be back. I can't think otherwise, or I'll go and change my mind and send someone else. I won't rest, my friend, until I see you back in camp unharmed. Now go."

Bubba went to his quarters, changed out of his uniform, and as he was putting on his civilian clothes, he glanced at the birthmark on his right leg. He thought back to the time he imagined he saw a similar one on Bill's leg. But now was not the time to think of such things, so he quickly finished dressing and went to join his men. When he arrived, he found them ready and waiting, with the others gathered around the wagon to wish them well. Richard walked over to Bubba and said, "You'd best get back here as quick as you can, otherwise I'll be forced to eat your portion of the neck bones and rice that I'm going to ask your mother to cook for us." Bubba smiled as he climbed into the wagon. "Don't worry, I'll be back in time to eat my share and some of yours, too." The men said their goodbyes and headed out determined to accomplish this very critical mission.

When they arrived in Folsom, Bubba pulled the wagon up behind an old run down shack located on the outskirts of town, where he knew the old man lived. It was funny that no one seemed to know his name; everyone had always referred to him as "the old man." Bubba knocked at the back door, and as it slowly opened the old man's face appeared.

He looked hard at Bubba, as if he were trying to recognize him. Bubba told him who he was, and pointed to his father sitting in the wagon. The old man looked at Louie and chuckled. "Yeah, I rememba you now; yo daddy could make a dead man laugh. Come on in, son, and tell me what brangs you here?" Bubba told him why they had come and how desperately they needed to know where the soldiers had gone. The old man looked at Bubba and smiled a toothless grin. "I figured them army folks was up to some funny business. When they found out them Yankees was comin, they started runnin round here like chickens with they heads cut off; the next day they packed up and left. One day you can't walk down the road without bumpin into one of them, the next day if they was payin a dollar for any you could find, you'd starve to death." Urgently Bubba said, "Beggin your pardon, Sir, but we got to move fast. Could you just tell me where they went?" "Show son, that's easy; they all gathered up there in Kingston." It made sense to Bubba. Kingston was close enough to Folsom for their plan to work like a charm. "There's just one more important thing I need to know. Do you have any idea how far the Yankees are from here?" "Show do son; day foe yestiday I heard one of them officers say that by Satday, which is today, ain't it?" "Yes sir, today is Saturday." "Well, then they should be camped bout a six-hour ride from here and it would most likely be Monday before they marched on Folsom, cause the way I sees it they got to take time to rest and plan they attack." "Thank you, sir, you may have just saved some lives by giving me this information." The old man stood at the door, watching them leave. "Go and take God with you, son. He gone take care of you cause you one of his own."

Bubba and his men waved goodbye to the old man and headed off in search of the Yankees. After riding for about four hours, they stopped to rest and eat. Bubba could tell that the men were getting a little nervous knowing that they were coming ever closer to the Yankee camp, so he gave them some instructions. "Men, when we get there, let me do all the talking; ya'll just sort of nod your heads and agree with what I say." Meatball said, "Don't worry, Lieutenant, we know what to do." Bubba sighed. "Meatball, whatever you do, don't call me Lieutenant! That goes for the rest of you, too; if you do, they'll most likely kill us where we stand. And daddy, when we get there I want you to stay close by the wagon, and especially our guns, because if things go wrong we're gonna have to haul our butts out of there like the devil himself was after us." "Don't worry son, if trouble starts, you best believe I bees ready." As soon as they were able, they were on the move again. A little over two hours into the second leg of their journey, Bubba spotted men on horseback coming toward them; as they came closer he realized they were Yankee soldiers and he could feel his heartbeat quicken. He suddenly knew that talking about what had to be done, and actually doing it, were two entirely different things. As the soldiers approached the wagon, he somehow managed to calm himself down. Their Sergeant said, "Where are you boys headed?" Bubba replied, eyes cast down, "Wees headed for our freedom, Captain." The Sergeant laughed and said, "I'm a Sergeant not a Captain. Do you understand?" Bubba, with a submissive look on his face said, "Yeah suh, Captain." The Sergeant rolled his eyes and said, "You boys been traveling long?" "Yeah suh, since bout daybreak this mornin." "Where are you looking to find your freedom?" the Sergeant asked, amused by these slaves. "We aims to look for somethin called the Underground Railroad and make it to the North," Bubba said, twisting his old, battered hat in his hands. "When my brother run away lookin for it he was headed this away, and he ain't nevah come back since that time, so we figures that he musta found it." "So what you're telling me is that you boys are runaway slaves?" No one answered the Sergeant. He finally said, "Its okay to tell me the truth. There are a lot of you slaves trying to make it to the North since the war started. Don't look so scared; you're among friends now, we'll help you along your way. How did you boys manage to sneak away?" "Evahbody so busy packin up to leave since they heard ya'll was comin, that they most likely ain't even missed us yet; all them soldiers left yestiday." What Bubba said about the soldiers got the Sergeant's immediate attention. "Listen to me carefully, boy; did you say that the soldiers have left Folsom?" "Yeah Suh, I show did, Captain." The Sergeant motioned to them. "You boys follow us into our camp; the Colonel needs to hear this."

As they entered the camp, Bubba and his men were shocked at the sight of so many soldiers. He thought to himself that Richard was definitely right when he said that attempting to fight this huge Yankee Army would be suicidal. The Sergeant stopped them in the middle of the camp, then dismounted and went into a large tent, which Bubba assumed was the Colonel's quarters. The soldiers paid little attention to them as they sat waiting for the Sergeant to return with his commanding officer. Suddenly, there was an obvious commotion coming from the tent, as the Colonel came out with the Sergeant at his heels. "Which man did you talk to, Sergeant?" The Sergeant pointed at Bubba. The Colonel said, "Bring him and some of the others to my quarters." Louie stayed with the wagon. Once inside, the Colonel asked Bubba to repeat what he said about the soldiers. Bubba told his story, practically word for word, and the others intentionally looked very frightened and nodded their heads in agreement. "What is your name?" "My name is Bubba, Suh." "Well, Bubba do you know where the soldiers went?" "Yeah Suh, they moved they camp to Kingston." "How many soldiers would you say they have?" Bubba answered, "I don't rightly know that, Suh, but they's a good many of them; it don't seem to me that they got too much stomach for fightin." The Colonel smiled and said, "Thank you very much Bubba, you men have done us a great service. Sergeant, see that these men are fed before you send them on their way."

The Yankee soldiers not only fed them well, but also had their cook give them a parcel of food to take with them. Once on the road again, Arthur said, "They was real nice to us. Kinda makes me wonder why nice folks like them want to take our home away from us." Bubba shrugged. "It's not their fault, they're following orders just the same as we are."

When Bubba figured he'd gone far enough, he found a path leading into the woods were he could hide the wagon and give himself a vantage point to spy on the Yankee soldiers. He had to have visual proof, that the plan to get them to split their forces had worked. It would be getting dark soon, so he decided that each man would take his turn as a lookout while the others got some sleep. If the soldiers were going to make a move, he knew it would be in the morning; only an idiot would attempt to move so many men at night through an unfamiliar area, and the Colonel did not strike him as an idiot.

Louie had taken the first watch, and as he sat there staring out into the darkness, he heard a noise and turned to see Bubba coming to join him. "How you holding up, daddy?" "I'm doin just fine son. I ain't as tough as I used to be, but I'm still all man. You know son, I was just sittin here thinkin of how I been proud of you since the day you was born; not that I don't love David and Jab, and God knows that Bee is my heart, but you always been kinda special. With the way thangs are movin so fast, it's gettin kinda hard to catch up with what's happenin in the world. A few weeks ago we was just slaves, now we soldiers in the Army and in a few days we'll be tryin to kill other soldiers, and they'll be tryin to kill us. Somehow it just don't make no sense." Louie took a deep breath. "Seems to me that white folks would have a better way of settlelin thangs than tryin to kill each other. We black folks are just caught in the middle. They reminds me of two wild dogs fightin over a piece of meat, and maybe that's all we is to them son, a piece of meat. What I'm tryin to say, Bubba, is that you brang lots of joy to my life, and if someone was to take that away, my life just won't be worth livin." Bubba had never heard his father talking so seriously before and it upset him. "Now, daddy," he said calmly, "stop worrying yourself for nothing. We all are going to come through this war just fine. We'll be joking, laughing and enjoying life and each other for years to come. You're just tired, so please get some sleep now and I'll stand watch for awhile." Bubba watched as Louie, without another word, crawled under some blankets. He vowed he would see his daddy acting like himself again when this war was over.

David had just taken over the morning watch when he noticed the Yankee camp starting to come alive. He motioned to the rest of the men and they all watched and waited to see if the performance they put on for the Yankees had worked. After about an hour's time there was a flurry of activity in the camp, tents were being taken down, wagons were being loaded with supplies, and their officers seemed to be barking out orders. Several hours later, they watched with satisfaction as the main body of soldiers marched out of camp headed toward Kingston. Bubba spoke for them all. "Well, I'll be damned, it worked! Now let's watch for a while longer and see how many they left behind." He finally estimated that there was a force of about four hundred soldiers remaining in the camp. He was positive they would be heading for Folsom by Monday morning, thinking that it would be theirs for the taking. "Well, men, it looks like the odds aren't quite even, but at least now we stand a fighting chance. Let's circle around them and get on back to our camp with the good news."

Spirits were so good on the trip back that Sammy and David started telling lies, and his daddy seemed more like his old self. Meatball asked, "David you still got that bottle of white folk's wine hidden somewhere? I think we all be willin to take a swig of it, cause if we make it back to camp, I be ready to take a swig of anythang." They all laughed, this being one of the rare times that they wholeheartedly agreed with him.

Suddenly, out of nowhere, three white men on horseback came galloping toward them. As they got closer, Bubba could see that they were definitely not soldiers; he sensed trouble in the making. He turned to the others, saying, "Something tells me that these men are up to no good, so ya'll have them guns at the ready, but keep them hidden because we don't want to invite trouble. I could be wrong about them, but we're taking no chances." Bubba stopped the wagon as the men rode up to them. "Show is a fine day ain't it, Suh?" "Well now, that depends on the answers you boys give us. Looks like you four bucks and that old man are pretty far from home. Ya'll wouldn't be runaway slaves now would you?" "No Suh," Bubba said respectfully, "We just on our way to Folsom to pick up some supplies for our Master." The man who seemed to be their leader, went on. "Well, I can see how that old man might need some help but just one of you big Bucks would be enough to help any man, young or old; I'd be willing to bet that your master paid a pretty penny for ya'll, ain't that right, boy?" Bubba slumped into his seat. "Suh, we don't mean no disrespect. We just tryin to do what our Master told us to, and he gone be mad if we late when we gits back." "Well boy," the man sniggered, let me tell you something; he's going to be even madder when ya'll don't come back at all." Bubba had heard about such men as these; they made a business of looking for slaves that had for whatever reason wandered too far from their master's domain. They rounded them up like stray cattle, intending to sell them to the highest bidder in a neighboring state. Pulling his revolver from its holster, the man pointed it at Bubba. "Pull this wagon into them woods over there and I mean right now, and don't do anything foolish; I can't get paid nothing for a dead slave." Bubba sat there looking into the barrel of the gun thinking, damn, this just could not be happening. Not now! He knew they had to do something and do it quick. The man waved his gun, threatening them all. "I see you boys need a little demonstration to show you just how serious I am. I can pick up another slave along the way to replace you, boy," he laughed, putting the gun to Bubba's head and cocking the hammer. Like a clap of thunder, a shot rang out. Bubba smelled the gunpowder and wondered why he felt no pain. With shocked surprise and relief, he saw a hole in the man's forehead, and blood trickling from it, as he toppled from his horse. The other two men, stunned by what had happened, were slow to react. He heard his father's voice. "I kill any son of a bitch that tries to take my son's, life." Bubba turned around and there stood his daddy taking deadly aim. But before Louie could fire again, Sammy and David cut loose on them with their revolvers, knocking them to the ground. The only shot fired by those men was when one of their guns discharged after they fell. Bubba grabbed a gun, saying to Sammy and Arthur, "Let's make sure those bastards are dead." There wasn't any question about it. They'd never see daylight again. As Bubba turned back toward the wagon, he saw a sight that sent shivers through his body; Meatball, holding his daddy in his arms. He rushed to the wagon only to discover that the stray bullet from the discharged gun had struck his daddy down. Bubba was shaking so much that he could barely climb into the wagon to hold his father, as blood poured from his chest. He remembered the words his daddy had spoken last night, and the tears started flowing. Oh my God, he thought, don't let this be happening, not my daddy, oh Lord, not my daddy! Louie motioned for Bubba to come closer as he whispered his last words, "I always be round to watch over you son, just like today." Bubba shook his father, then held him tightly, begging him, choking on the words spilling out. "Daddy please, stay with me! Don't leave me, daddy!" Quietly sobbing, cradling his daddy's head against his chest, he whispered, "I love you, daddy", as Louie took his last breath.

CHAPTER FIFTEEN

Back at the training camp, Bill and Richard were pleased that all the men reported back as scheduled; they would spend the weekend practicing the fighting tactics that they would be using against the enemy. Richard hoped that the extra training would help boost their confidence. Sgt. Kimbro was instructed to have them practice not only the proper way to fire their weapon, but also how it was to be used in close combat. This was to be done repeatedly until he was positive that each man knew how to handle his weapon properly, under any circumstances.

The evening hour was fast approaching as Richard sat in Bill's quarters looking at his troubled face. "Don't worry, Bill, Bubba will be returning soon." "Am I that obvious?" "Yes Sir, you sure are." Bill stared off into space, thinking out loud. "Bubba and I have always behaved like brothers rather than Master and slave. Just thinking about him being in harm's way upsets and worries me; if anything should happen to him it would be very difficult to carry on. We've always been together; I can't imagine life without him." Richard realized that Bill was verbalizing his thoughts and not really talking to him, so he offered no reply.

At that moment, Bubba's brother Jab came running into Bill's tent. "Beggin your pardon, Captain, but they's comin." Bill snapped out his reverie. "Who's coming?" "Bubba and the men, they's here." Bill got to his feet so fast he didn't even remember standing up; he ran out of the tent and immediately saw Meatball driving the wagon into the camp. As he hurriedly walked to the wagon he saw Bubba sitting in the back holding his father. "Oh my God, Bubba, what happened?" Bubba told him everything that had happened from the time they left camp. "If I had insisted that he stay in camp he'd be alive now." Taking Bubba's arm, Bill spoke quietly. "Bubba, I grieve with you, but please don't blame yourself for this; for some reason only God knows, he chooses certain people to get a glimpse into the future, and I believe your father was such a person. He went on that mission feeling a strong need to protect his son, and I am positive that at this very moment God is saying to him, "Well done soldier, mission accomplished." Bubba looked at Bill with tears in his eyes. "There are no words to describe the pain I feel, I keep hoping that he's just playing one of his jokes and will wake up any minute now." The men had slowly gathered around the wagon and offered their sympathies to Bubba and his brothers. Louie was a man who was liked as well as loved, and many hearts would be heavy with missing him.

Bill ordered Sgt. Kimbro to assign some men to prepare Louie's body, dressing him in the uniform he never got to wear, but so gallantly earned. He placed his hand on Bubba's shoulder. "Now, my friend, I know that you and your brothers must prepare for the even more painful task of taking your father home to your mother; I pray that God will give her the strength to endure this tragic moment in her life." Bubba nodded. "We'll bury him at sun up, he really loved that time of the day, said it always made him feel so peaceful. He used to tell us that it was the best time to talk to God, before he got busy with everybody else."

Bubba drove the wagon up to the cabin just as his mama was coming outside. "Lord be praised! Ya'll made it back safe and sound. Lt. Roach told me not to worry myself none, he come ovah and had supper with us Fridiy night; that man show can eat." Alice suddenly realized she was the only one talkin. "Why ya'll so quiet? And where's that big mouth man of mine?" When her sons did not answer her, she went on, "Don't tell me he done gone and got sick. I told that fool he was too old to be runnin round tryin to play soldier, now I got to go to that camp and tend to his needs. I swear ya'll men is somethin; ya'll would bust hell wide open befoe you listen to a woman." With a chill running down her spine, Alice nervously asked, "How come ya'll ain't talkin? He is sick, ain't he?" Bubba climbed down from the wagon, walked over to his mama and as he started to put his arms around her, he started sobbing. Her whole body stiffening, she questioned her son. "What done happen Bubba?" He could not find the words to tell his mama that his daddy was dead, so he gently guided her to the back of the wagon. When she saw Louie lyin there, dead, she screamed, "Oh Jesus, not my Louie! Oh Lord Jesus, not my Louie!" And threw herself on his body, uncontrollably sobbing. Bee, hearin all the commotion ran out of the cabin to see what was going on; the sight of her daddy lyin in the wagon with her mama sprawled on top of him, was too much to bear. Bee screamed only once, then fainted.

It was a glorious sunrise, as if God had outdone Himself to honor Louie. Everyone in the slave quarters had turned out to attend Louie's funeral. Brother Barrow finished his eulogy by saying, "Lord, we hate to interrupt you cause we knows you is busy laughin at Louie's jokes, but we want to say thank you for takin our brother into your mansion; he will serve you well up there in heaven just like he served you here.

Amen." A strong, but sad "Amen" echoed back from the crowd.

Bubba heard the sound of men singing, and as he turned he saw Bill and Richard leading the militia unit dressed in full uniform to the grave site, singing Dixie. They filed past the family saluting, some with tears in their eyes; no words were necessary. His father had died a heroic death and these men were honoring him. Bubba's heart swelled with pride at this moving tribute to his brave and well-loved daddy.

When it came time for Bubba and his family to leave the cemetery, the thought of his father being left there alone tormented him. He knew it had to be done, but he was having a great deal of trouble accepting it. Putting his arm around his mama, they slowly walked home consoling each other along the way.

The next morning Bubba and his brothers returned to camp. He headed straight for Bill's quarters where he found both Bill and Richard making plans for the next day's anticipated attack by the Yankees. They were surprised to see that he had returned so soon after his father's funeral. With concern in his voice Bill asked, "We did not expect you back this early, is everything all right?" "There was nothing more I could do at home, Bill, and I think mama really wanted to be alone for awhile. If she needs anything,

Bee is there to see after her." "Bubba, if there is anything I can do to help, you know all you have to do is name it!" Bubba's lips attempted a smile. "Just keep being the friend that you've always been." "I can promise you I'll be that friend for the rest of my life," Bill responded. "Is that good enough?" Bubba looked at Bill and tried to answer like his old self would. "I'll have to think about it." Richard walked over to them. "Welcome back, Bubba, I've missed you a great deal." "It's good to be back, Richard, and I want to thank you for looking in after my mama while I was away." "The pleasure was all mine Bubba. Your mother's cooking sure beats this Army food," he replied with a smile.

Bill motioned to Bubba. "Come over here, Bubba, and take a look at these rough drawings we've made of the areas we'll be defending." Bubba carefully examined them and said, "These drawings show that you think the Yankees will be passing near our camp on the way to Folsom!" Bill nodded. "That's what Richard and I hope will happen because it would be to our advantage to try and hold them here, rather than fight them in the large areas of open space surrounding Folsom. There is no way we can fight them head on, they would cut us to pieces. The protection of woods that line the roads here would allow us to strike them using the hit and run tactics that's been a major part of our training. If we get lucky enough and they decide to take this approach, we can fight them on our terms." Before Bubba could reply, Sgt. Kimbro came rushing into the tent saying, "Excuse me, Captain, but the scouts I sent out this morning have returned." "That's excellent, Sergeant, let's hope they have some good news for us; show them in." As the two scouts entered, Bill eagerly asked, "Well, gentlemen, were you able to determine what those Yankees are up to?" "Sir, it seems that they are definitely headed this way, but the thing is there seems to be more than the four hundred or so soldiers we figured on; we've estimated the force to consist of around five hundred men. We also think they'll be resting up soon and will probably continue on their way at daybreak, which means pretty much as we already figured, they'll be passing through here early tomorrow morning." Bill considered this information before responding. "That Yankee Colonel is no fool, he probably had second thoughts about the number of men he left behind and decided to reinforce them; thank you gentlemen, you've done a fine job."

Bill turned his attention back to Richard and Bubba. "Well, it seems as though we have our answer. Although their troop strength has been increased, the fact still remains that they don't know we're here. I say we take advantage of the element of surprise and cut their force down to size a bit." Startled, Bubba asked, "You mean we're going on the offensive and attack them

Tommie Thompson

first?" "That's exactly what I mean, Lieutenant. We'll attack them in force, killing as many of them as possible, then retreat back to the woods. They'll have no choice but to come after us; and that's when we employ our hit and run tactics. Of course, I'm open to any suggestions that you two might have to offer!" "Your strategy makes good sense and I'm sure Richard agrees with me, but I guess for me its just that we've been talking about and planning how to kill men for some time now, and knowing that tomorrow I must finally face the reality of it, makes me think of the last conversation I had with my daddy. After all this killing is done, I hope I can make some sense out of the whole thing." "Bubba, I really don't think that making sense of this war will be done in our lifetime; we must do what must be done now, and pray that God forgives us. Lt. Roach, I would like you to take these drawings to your quarters and come up with some strategic points of attack; we three will meet later with the sergeant and work out the details."

After Richard left, Bubba turned to Bill. "I know that you have something else on your mind Bill, now what is it?" "Oh, its just that I've been thinking that if worse comes to worse the plantation will be our last line of defense, and I feel uneasy about putting the lives of the men's families in jeopardy. Perhaps now is the time to give them the opportunity to leave; we could outfit them with supplies and have them make a camp somewhere out of harm's way until this is over. What do you think?" "That makes a lot of sense, Bill. I've been thinking along those same lines and I know that it would be easier on all of us when the fighting starts to know that our loved ones are relatively safe. But if we should lose this battle, I dread to think of what would become of them." "Bubba, I have given that considerable thought and the only solution that I can come up with, is you!" "And just what do you mean by that, Bill?" Bill raised an eyebrow. "Now, don't play dumb with me, Bubba. You remember we had a similar conversation a little more than a month ago, and the time is fast approaching when that plan may have to be implemented. If the worse should happen, they'd need a strong leader to help them make it to the North. I can think of no better man to perform that task than you. I'm sure you understand, Bubba, that if something should happen to me, they would be scattered and sold to the highest bidders, but by leading them North they stand a good chance of remaining together and starting over as free people. Although it would not be the type of freedom we planned, at least it would still be freedom. Although you already have your freedom, the papers still remain in my desk drawer, which gives your family their freedom, as well. There is also enough money to help take care of the needs you will incur along the way and to help everyone get established.

Now, promise me that if I should fall in battle, you will do as I have requested. I know we've talked about this before; I just want to set my mind at rest."

Bubba felt he had to question Bill about his sudden pessimism. "Why are you talking and acting like you're not going to be around much longer, Bill? We haven't even fought the damn Yankees yet and you're talking about dying?" "Okay Bubba, here's the truth. I had that dream again, you know the one I mean where the Angel of Death is riding towards me on horseback, only this time he's waving a sword that glimmers in the sunlight." "It's only a dream, Bill. We're all nervous about tomorrow and it's true that some men will die, but when the smoke clears you'll be standing there as glad to be alive as the rest of us that survive. Today I buried my daddy, and I don't care to think about the possibility of losing my best friend. Stop all this talk about your dying and spend more time thinking about living. Now, I'm with you, I think it's a wise move to prepare for the evacuation of our people, but somehow I don't think they'll go for it, even though we both agree that it's the best course of action. I'm not surprised at your concerns for their needs and safety, because I know these people are like family to you. I'll ride back to the plantation this afternoon and talk to everyone about what we've said here, but I can tell you right now that although my daddy is lying dead in his grave, mama ain't about to leave him and I'll bet you a twenty dollar gold piece that no one else is going to leave their loved ones at a time like this. When they said all of us or none of us, they meant exactly that, even if it means dying together."

After leaving Bill, Bubba went to his quarters and found Richard working feverishly on his assigned task. He stopped and looked up at Bubba. "Well, are you mentally prepared for tomorrow's action?" "I guess I'm as ready as I'll ever be, but it's not me I'm worried about, it's Bill. The weight of responsibility is taking its toll on him, so we must find every way possible to help him." "I agree with you, Bubba, but knowing that lives hang in the balance based on every decision you make is never an easy thing to do when you're in command; the best thing that we can do is to show support for his decisions, that way he won't feel as if he is making them entirely alone." "Yes, I suppose you're right, Richard, its just hard for me to watch him agonizing over situations that he has very little control over, such as the one I'm being sent to resolve now." Bubba then told him of the planned trip back to the plantation and the purpose. Richard smiled saying, "Bubba, I think that you're about to win a twenty dollar gold piece because your assumption is absolutely correct." "Well, in any case, I need to change into some comfortable clothes for the trip back, this uniform is killing me; be a friend and help me get these boots off." As he was helping Bubba, Richard noticed something. "That's odd." "What's odd?" "This birthmark on your leg. I was in Bill's quarters the other day when he was changing clothes and unless my eyes are playing tricks on me, he has a birthmark that's identical to this one, and it's also on his right leg. In all these years together haven't the two of you ever noticed it?" Bubba did not tell Richard that he had noticed it years ago when he saved Bill from being bitten by a snake, and that he, too, thought his eyes were playing tricks on him; instead, he replied, "I guess sometimes it takes a stranger to point out the obvious." Then he made light of it by saying, "I don't suppose my daddy was sneakin around in the big house when he was a young man," which made them both laugh. " Enough about birthmarks, I need to get started so that I'll be back in time for our strategy meeting."

As Bubba rode toward the plantation his mind was running wild trying to come up with explanations for the fact that he and Bill had the same birthmark. He found himself thinking about things that never occurred to him before now. He had not given any particular thought to the fact that his features and skin tone seemed more that of a white man than black. But no one in the slaves quarters ever said anything or teased him when he was young, and as far as he could recall, not one member of his family had ever brought it up. This was the first time he had ever considered this strange behavior on the part of everyone. He thought back to when he was a boy and recalled how his family had always received special attention from Bill's father; could there have been a reason for such kindness? He suddenly felt ashamed for having such thoughts. It wasn't right to dishonor the memory of his daddy, nor to indulge in disrespectful thoughts about his mama, because he knew that's exactly where these thoughts were heading. But he couldn't control his excitement at the possibility that he and Bill might be brothers, and that long ago there could have been a pact made to conceal his real parentage. And what would be the consequences of finding out the truth? With everything that happened in the past few days, Bubba was sure now was not the best time to bring old secrets out into the open. He knew he would have to wait patiently to seek answers to this puzzle; answers that could bring both joy and pain.

When he finally looked in on his mama and informed her why he was back so soon, she said, "I don't know bout them other folks Bubba, but don't waste your breath tryin to talk me into goin no where, cause I ain't goin and that's that." He smiled and hugged his mama. "I already figured as much, mama. Let me get on over to the big house and ring the bell, no sense putting off telling the other folks what the situation is and letting them choose how they want to handle it. I'll come back and spend a little more time with you before I return to camp." Alice replied, "You know son, the Lord show know what he's doin, you've been heavy on my mind all day and I feel like he sent you back here to lift a burden from me." Bubba felt a churning in the pit of his stomach, as he said nervously, "Mama, what on earth are you talking about?" "It says in the Bible, son, that what you do in the darkness will one day come to the light, and that the truth shall set you free. With all my heart, I want to be free when I meet my maker." The last thing Bubba wanted was to put his mama through more anguish, so soon after the death of his daddy, so he held her close, and made an attempt at changing the conversation. "Mama, stop talkin like this, you ain't going to die no time soon and we'll all be free one day, just like I promised." Alice shook her head vigorously. "I'm not talkin bout that kind of freedom, son, I'm talkin bout the kind of freedom you feel deep down in your soul when you know you done got right with God. Now you go on and take care of business; we'll have us a long talk when you come back."

Bubba fought the strong urge to remain and hear her out. Every instinct in his body, told him, the truth concerning his birth and upbringing, would be answered this very day! And the words that would confirm his suspicion of being the illegitimate son of Bill's father would come from his mama's lips. But he also realized, he had to calm down and let her tell it, in her own way. He walked to the big house, deep in thought. My whole life seems to be turning upside down in one day. I know my mama is a good woman, she's always gone out of her way to help others, and no one could ask for a better mama. I know the things she wants to tell me with such urgency, will come from more than just the shock of my daddy's death. Growing tired of speculating, Bubba picked up his pace. He was anxious to return to his mama, and hear the truth about his real father. But no truth revealed could change the fact that Louie would always be his daddy!

Bubba rang the bell and watched as people quickly gathered, everyone anxious to hear any news of the war. He did not mince words, he shared the conversation he and Bill had concerning their safety should the battle extend to the plantation grounds. Then he asked for a show of hands. "How many of you are willing to take your chances and try to make it to the North?" Hattie's sister Rosa spoke up and said, "I ain't gone leave Arthur here alone, God knows that man couldn't take care of hisself when they weren't no war, so I know he'll need me now. I just couldn't stand the thought of him lyin somewhere hurt or dyin without me bein there to comfort him." All of the other women agreed with her by saying, "You is speakin the truth, sister, cause we all gone stand by our men folk." Old man Barrow stepped forward. "Bubba, it looks like ya'll gone be stuck with us, all we can do is put our faith in the Lord to see us through this terrible time, because no matter what we decide, He has the final say." Bubba thanked them for their show of love and support, and then eagerly headed back home to be with his mother, his thoughts racing. Was he going to find out at last why once again, seeing that shared birthmark brought questions he had never asked before?

Bubba entered the cabin and found his mama sitting at the kitchen table; he was pleased to see that she was up and around. "I see you're feeling a bit better, mama?" "Yes, son, I was just thinkin bout your daddy and what a good man he was; you know I didn't love your daddy when we first married. I guess Master Bill's daddy didn't know that he was helpin to do the work of the Lord when he chose him for me, cause that man loved me sometin fierce, and when you was born he took to you like you was his own." Bubba attempted to speak, but she shushed him. "Please don't say anythang, son, until I'm finished talkin; I've been carryin this burden a long time and I need to unload it while God give me the strength to do it. Your daddy dyin like he did reminds me of how death can come so suddenly to any one of us. I've tried to live my life in a way that I be ready to meet my Maker any time he chooses to take me, but I don't want to leave here without makin thangs right. Alice sighed and clasped her hands together. "Evah time I sees you and Master Bill together my heart just aches. I been feelin the spirit of your daddy tellin me to do somethin neither one of us had the courage to do when he was alive." Bubba took her hands in his. "What's that mama?" he asked softly. "Tell you the truth, Bubba, and I hope you find it in your heart to forgive us for makin you live a lie."

Alice quietly began telling her story with tear-filled eyes. She took him back to the time when she was but a girl who suddenly found herself in bed with the Master, and how after a number of these times she became with child. She painfully told him how and why Bill's father covered up the result of his indiscretion. She had no choice but to agree with his plan. With tears now running down her face she said, "When you was born, your daddy took you, held you in his arms, and he hugged and kissed you. I knew right then that I could learn to love a man who could show so much love for a child not of his own blood. From the day you was born and till the day he died, he nevah treated you like he wasn't your father. I saw that man show so much love for you that for a while I thought he was just doin what the Master wanted, but then I say to myself, can't nobody order no one to show the kind of love I saw in his eyes evah time he looked at you. Louie may not have been your real father, but he was sure the best daddy that you could have ever asked for." Alice continued, voice trembling, "I saw right from the start that you and Master Bill took to each other like two peas in a pod. It was a wonder to me that ya'll nevah noticed that you two had the same strawberry-lookin birthmarks on your right leg, just like the Master. You said yoself that it seemed that ya'll was meant to be friends; like some strange force was pullin ya'll together. That strange force is the blood bond you two share as brothers, and the Lord tryin to work thangs out. Bubba, I just can't go on livin with this heavy on my heart, knowin that one or both of ya'll could be killed tomorrow without evah knowing the truth; lettin it come out in the light is the only way I can free all of us from the sins of the past."

Bubba put his arms around his mama and hugged her for dear life. "Mama, I can forgive you anything. It's not myself that I'm thinking about at this moment. The thought of how you and daddy have been burdened with this secret all these years…." He could not continue because the tears started running down his cheeks, as he held his mother tighter, vowing, "I'll always love you and daddy, mama. Nothing that happened in the past could ever change that." Alice knew he spoke the truth and thanked the Lord for it. He was still, and would always be, her loving son.

CHAPTER SIXTEEN

The sun was going down when Bubba returned to the camp, his emotions running high. He and Bill had jokingly called each other brother for years, and now the truth of the matter was that they really were. He had to honor his mama's wishes and tell Bill the secret that had been well hidden since the day they were born. All during the trip back he had been trying to figure out just how to go about doing that. He finally decided that there was no easy way to turn a man's life upside down, he would simply take the same approach that his mother did in telling him; just come straight out with the truth and pray to almighty God that the bond between them would provide the strength needed to accept their blood brotherhood.

Bill was sitting at his small makeshift desk when Bubba came in. Looking up he said, "I was just thinking that it was getting close to the time for you to return. "Tell me, how did it go?"

"Bubba held out his hand, palm up. "You owe me a twenty dollar gold piece." Bill smiled. "Well, seeing that you didn't have a twenty dollar gold piece in the first place, I'd say that makes us even!" Bubba laughed as he reached inside his pants pocket and pulled out a twenty dollar gold piece, and slammed it on the desk, "Pay up." Bill picked up the coin. "You sly dog, where in the hell did you get that?" "This may come as a shock to you, Bill, but your father gave it to me on my sixteenth birthday and made me promise not to tell anyone about it; he said it was a gift not only for my birthday but because I deserved it." "You know, Bubba, it amazed me how father really seemed to take a liking to you right from the start, but what a strange thing for him to say." Bubba tapped his gold piece on the desk. "Now, if you'll kindly match this one with one out of your pocket, I'll have two gold pieces. But this time, I'm telling everybody." They both had a good hearty laugh as Bill thought how good it felt to see Bubba back in good spirits again.

"Bill, you know how sometimes as an adult engaged in general conversation, someone can say something that jolts your memory, and your mind takes you back to the past when you were a child? And then you begin to recall certain things that happened which didn't make much sense to you at the time, but now suddenly looking back on them as an adult, they began to make perfect sense?" "Yes, Bubba, I know exactly what you mean, but what are you getting at?" Bubba took a deep breath. "I haven't thought much about those words your father said to me in years, the same way I didn't pay a lot of attention to the special treatment he seemed to give me and my family. I never questioned it, I just assumed it was because we were friends; almost like brothers." "Well, your assumption was right on target Bubba, deep down inside my father knew we were inseparable and would always be like brothers." Bubba shifted nervously in his chair. "Bill, do you have any brandy hidden anywhere in this tent?" "I sure do, Bubba, but I don't think it's wise for you to start drinking with all the planning left to be done." "It's not for me, Bill, it's for you." Bill looked very surprised. "Bubba, what makes you think I need a drink?" "Just trust me, Bill, and pour yourself a damn drink. What the hell, pour me one, too." Bill found the bottle of brandy and poured two glasses, handing one to Bubba, "Now tell me, my friend, just what are we drinking to?" Bubba raised his glass. "To you, the brother I never knew I had." "What's that supposed to mean? We've always been as close as any two brothers could be, and you know that! So what are we toasting?" Bubba stared hard at Bill, the moment had come. "Because today, Bill, I found out that we really are true brothers," he said, downing his drink, and then pulling up his pants, exposing the strawberry birthmark. Bill took one look and knew Bubba had spoken the truth. That birthmark was like a brand among male members of the Shields family. With a shock he thought, how on earth could I have not noticed it before? Without saying a word, he turned up his drink, and looked at Bubba as if he were seeing him for the first time. "Well, I'll be damned. I had no reason to look for him in you before, but I see it now; clear as day. This means you're the one, Bubba, it was right in front of my face all this time, and I never caught on." Bubba looked puzzled. "What do mean, I'm the one?" "When I was a child I overheard my father and his manservant Bernard talking in his study. Curious, I decided to eavesdrop on their conversation, but unfortunately I came in on the tail end of it so what I heard was, "Bernard, you must talk to your friends in the slave quarters and find out who is starting rumors concerning that boy's real father, and put an end to it." I thought that Bernard had gotten himself into some real trouble and that my father was trying to help him get out of it. I've given no significance to the matter until right now," Bill said, a strange expression on his face. "Bubba, other than the birthmark, is there any other proof that this is really true?" "The best proof in the world, Bill; my mama's word." For a moment, Bill was speechless. "My God, Bubba, I just don't know what to say." "Don't say anything, Bill, until I've finished. My mama just told me the entire story, with tears running down her cheeks. Believe me, it took all the courage she could muster up to tell it, but because of the war, she knew we both had to hear it."

When Bubba had finished Bill said, with deep distress and anger in his voice. "For the first time in my life I feel ashamed of my father; that he could have done such a thing and gone to such lengths to cover it up, is unforgivable. I've spent my whole life believing my father was a good, God-fearing man, now I find out that he was no better than those other slave-owning bastards who take slave women for their sexual pleasure without giving it a second thought." Bubba interrupted him then, saying, "Wait a minute Bill, there's more to this story you haven't heard yet. Your father cared enough to place two people together who would properly care for me, and my daddy and mama raised me with all the love and caring that anyone could ask for, and your father didn't just cast my mama aside. I'll never know what his true feelings were, but I do know that my mama learned to care for him a great deal, perhaps even loved him. As I listened to her tell her story, at first, I too, was outraged, but then my anger began to melt away. I could hear there was no hate or ill will in her voice toward your father; there was only a quiet understanding of what took place long ago, and a deep remorse at having to keep the truth from me. If she found it in her heart to forgive him, who are we to do otherwise? Being angry or hating won't change a thing. We have to accept what happened in the past, look for the good that came out of it, and think about the future." Bill looked at his best friend, and now, real brother, with tears in his eyes. "All these years of pretending to be brothers and suddenly finding out that we really are, is mind-boggling. Bubba, I am thrilled to find out that we really are brothers, but at the same time, it feels like I'm condoning the actions of my father. All of this is so confusing and unexpected; you have to agree it will take some time getting used to the idea." "No, I don't think so, Bill, because we've never treated each other as if we weren't brothers. Don't you see? This explains why we had this powerful desire to become friends when we first met, and feel sort of lost when we're apart for too long. Hell, man, most times we even think alike! Of course, I'm a little smarter than you, but you've learned to live with that." Bill couldn't help but laugh. "Louie may not have been your real father, but you sure have his sense of humor." "That's exactly what I'm trying to say, Bill. The people who loved us and raised us, and be it right or wrong in the eyes of others, did what they felt they had to in order to protect us." "You're right, Bubba, and when this battle is over, I will promise your mother that we will no longer just act like brothers, but we'll live like brothers; they'll be no more secrets. I feel no shame at having you in my family. In fact, I'm very proud to call you my blood brother." "I had no doubt you'd feel this way Bill, same as I do. I'm looking forward to the day when we can openly acknowledge our kinship."

The sight of seeing two men hugging when he entered Bill's quarters startled Richard so much that he was speechless. Bubba and Bill laughed at the expression on Richard's face. "What's the matter Lieutenant, haven't you ever seen two brothers hugging before?" Bubba asked. "Don't tell me that my suspicions were correct! This morning you seemed to make light of the similarities in those birthmarks, but I had a strong feeling that there was more to it than just coincidence. It's fascinating and ironic that you discovered this all in one day. How in the world did you manage that?" Bubba gave him a brief version of his mama's story. "I find your story sad, yet in the end, beautiful. I guess there really is something to a phrase I've heard your people using a lot." "Which phrase is that, Richard?" "If I remember correctly, that God may not come when you call Him, but He's always on time. And it seems to me, that today His timing was perfect. And now, Captain, I hate to be the one to put a damper on a wonderful occasion, but the fact is that we must get busy with the completion of our plan of attack for tomorrow." "You're absolutely correct, Lieutenant; get Sgt. Kimbro, we'll start planning our strategy at once."

Darkness was beginning to fall as they completed their meeting. Bill asked the Sergeant to get the men into formation; he would speak to them one more time before the fighting started to give them words of encouragement that might help to conquer the fear he knew they all were feeling.

Most of the men who stood before him had been transformed from slaves into soldiers, and he could tell by the look of pride in their eyes that they considered themselves to be men; men who were no longer willing to cower and settle for being referred to as "boys." Only time would tell if they would be able to pass this legacy on to other slaves in the South, but at least tomorrow these men would make their mark in history.

Bill shared these thoughts with the men, seeing their chests swell as a feeling of pride flowed through them. He also felt a need to tell the men the personal discovery made today, the fact that he and Bubba were actually blood brothers. Gazing with great pride and respect at this crowd, he said, "Men, there is only one way to say this, so I'll say it straight out. Today I found out that Lt. Shields and I are brothers by blood, and no man could ask for a finer one. When my father died he left me with land and money, but none of that compares to the well kept secret and wonderful gift that I discovered today." A loud cheer came up from the men, at hearing this news. David spoke up. "Beggin your pardon, Captain, but Jab and me knowed it all the time. We heard an old midwife who been long since dead, talkin bout it one day when we was just boys; even mama and daddy didn't know that we knew. We sneaked over to the barn to steal us a little homebrew that we knowed the growed folks kept in there. That old lady didn't know we was in there gettin drunk, when she started runnin off at the mouth to another lady bout it. We done told a lot of thangs since that day, but we ain't nevah got drunk enough to tell that to nobody." Bubba laughed. "And all this time I though ya'll was crazy; hell, ya'll had good sense, after all!" Sammy, not to be outdone, yelled, "Hey, Arthur, seein that it's fessin up time, why don't you tell us bout them two pickaninie's runnin round the plantation lookin like you spit them out, but you swearin ain't yo's?" Everyone laughed, as Richard looked on, amazed at their ability to find humor in just about everything that life handed out. Sgt. Kimbro, laughing as hard as anyone, dismissed the men, as they continued to poke fun at one another. This was definitely not the military way of doing things, but what the hell! He knew that many of these men would be killed or wounded tomorrow, so why not let them enjoy these last light-hearted moments of fun together.

Bill turned to Richard and Bubba saying, "What do you say we head back to my quarters and follow the men's lead; we'll talk about pleasant times in our lives for awhile and maybe even share a bottle of brandy?" Neither answered him, they just started running toward his tent and left him standing there. When Bill entered his quarters they were sitting on his cot partaking of his excellent brandy. Looking at him with big grins, Bubba said, "What took you so long?" Bill laughed along with them. "Give me that bottle before I take it and brain both of you with it." Sitting around telling jokes and sharing humorous episodes from their lives, Bubba knew that they were all dreading the coming of dawn and secretly wishing this night could last forever. Finally, Bill stood up saying, "Well, gentlemen, as much as I hate for this to end, we have only a few hours left before daylight, so I suggest we try and get a little sleep, but before we do, let's pray that our dreams don't turn into nightmares." Bubba and Richard said, "Amen to that," and quietly left the tent.

CHAPTER SEVENTEEN

The sound of a bugle instantly woke Bubba from his sleep. As he was getting dressed, there was an undeniable feeling of unease thinking about the events this day would bring. He looked at Richard, also in the process of getting dressed, and said, "Well, I guess this is it?" Richard nodded. "Yes, I'm afraid so, Bubba. Take my advice and don't dwell on it, because once you fire that first shot it becomes a matter of survival; they'll be time enough to feel remorse for your actions when the battle is over. Right now, the first order of the day is to get some good breakfast."

A short while later, when they entered Bill's quarters, Sgt. Kimbro was already there giving Bill the position of the Yankee soldiers. "Good morning gentlemen," Bill greeted them. "As you no doubt heard, the Sergeant has done a fantastic job of keeping up with the whereabouts of the Yankees. We'll stick to our plan and deploy the men on both sides of the road leading past here, using the woods for cover. When we get them in our sights, those Yankees will be in for a big surprise. Get the men ready, Sergeant." As they were leaving the tent, Bubba stopped and turned to look at Bill, thinking, this could be the last time we see each other alive. As if he were reading Bubba's mind Bill said, "Don't worry, my friend, we're going to come through this." They marched several miles down the road and deployed the men; Richard and Sgt. Kimbro commanding one side, leaving Bill and Bubba with the other. All they could do now was play a waiting game.

Bubba walked among the men giving them words of encouragement, and stopping at the position where his brothers and men close to his heart were assigned. He noticed that Meatball was looking nervous and strained. "How are you holding up, Meatball?" "Bubba, I don't rightly know for sure. I ain't nevah been fraid to fight no man, but today I'm shamed to say, that I'm really scared, and so is the rest of the men, cause today we gone be fightin white men and you know that don't come natural to us." Bubba looked around at all the men gathered there. "You men listen up. It's true we've never raised our hand to a white man and God knows there have been times when we wanted to. The only thing that stopped us was the fear of what would happen to our families, and us, if we did;

we saw other men try it and they ain't among us no more. Well, I'm here to tell you that the past is over and this is a new day. Today, we gone stand up and be men. We're now trained soldiers and we gone kill any son of a bitch that comes marchin down that road bent on fightin us, and we don't care what color his skin is cause we gone send him to meet his Maker before he sends us to meet ours. Now, men, raise your hand if you're with me," Bubba said, making a tight fist with his right hand, pointing straight up in the air. As all hands were raised to the sky, Meatball felt his courage return. Bubba put his arm around Meatball and whispered, "We 're all counting on each other today, and there's not a finer man that I'd rather have with me than you." As he turned to walk back to his assigned position Meatball said, "Thank you, Bubba, who woulda evah thought we'd turn out to be friends." "I truly believe that God thought about it, Meatball."

The order soon came down from Bill for all the men to be silent and at the ready; the Yankee soldiers were approaching and no one was to fire until he gave the order. As the column of soldiers marched confidently along the road and came into firing range, the men nervously waited for the order to fire. Bill knew that once he gave that order, the course of his life and that of his men would be changed forever. The cards had been dealt. He silently prayed that they held the winning hand, as he gave the order. Guns were fired; men were yelling, running and screaming; all hell seemed to break loose. Bill could hardly hear himself think, bombarded by the horrific sound of chaos all around him. The Yankee soldiers were dumbfounded as they watched their comrades falling to the ground beside them. All they saw were white puffs of smoke coming from the woods that surrounded them. They began to retreat, frantically, blindly, firing their weapons into the woods where the ambush was taking place.

Bubba could hear the bullets whistling through the trees and the sound of men screaming as some of them found their mark. His men, firing and reloading rifles as fast as they could, attempted to inflict as much damage on the enemy as possible. Glancing around quickly, he saw that several men had been hit, and he immediately thought of Bill. Bubba was filled with relief to see him still standing shouting orders to the men nearest him. Finally, the Yankees were able to move back out of firing range and took refuge in the woods surrounding that area. All firing came to an abrupt stop, the sudden silence almost frightening. No one said a word, they just looked at the dead and wounded soldiers sprawled in the road, and at their own comrades, wounded or killed. Remorse as well as guilt, washed over them, as they thanked God for somehow still being alive. Bubba, realizing that the shooting was over for now, gave orders to attend to those wounded. "Check to see who and how many of our men have been wounded or killed." With a heavy heart, he asked for a count of the wounded and the dead.

Bill appeared at Bubba's side. "Men, you have done a fine job this morning, you did exactly as you were trained to do and I'm proud of you, but the fighting is far from over. These Yankees are not going to give up that easily. Yes, we've made a real dent in their numbers, but they're going to come at us with all the force they can muster; so stay alert. Lt. Shields, do we know what our situation is yet?" "I'm having that checked on now, Sir." "Good. In the meantime, I'll make arrangements to have our wounded taken back to the plantation to receive proper medical attention. Thank God I had Miss Rosa trained as a nurse and she's a damn good one, but I never figured she'd be using her skills this way. I'll have the dead taken in a separate wagon for a proper burial." At that moment, the private assigned the task of making a list of the casualties, reported back saying, "There are twenty men wounded and eight men have been killed." Stone faced, Bill asked, "And Lt. Roach?" The private replied, "He's fine, Sir, and Lt. Shields brothers are fine, too." Bubba let out his breath. "Thank you, private, I needed to hear that." The private saluted. "You're quite welcome, Sir."

Bill turned to Bubba, seeing his own relief mirrored in Bubba's eyes. "Lt. Shields, I want you to locate Lt. Roach. Both of you will ride out with an armed escort under a flag of truce. Tell the Yankee commander that we'll hold our fire while he removes his dead and wounded from the road." "Yes Sir, I'll see to that immediately." Bill was thinking that not only was it the humane thing to do, but it would also buy some time to decide on his next plan of attack.

On his way to locate Richard, Bubba saw Meatball and noticed blood coming from what appeared to be a head wound. "How badly are you hurt?" Bubba asked with concern. "Ain't nothin but a scratch, Lieutenant, that bullet just bounced off my head. If they want to kill me they gone have to find another spot to shoot me; my mama always said I was hard-headed." Bubba shook his head, laughed, and continued on his way. After finding Richard they picked four men to escort them; a makeshift flag was made out of material that was to be used as bandages for the wounded.

Richard assured Bubba and the others that it was safe to enter the area where the Yankees were regrouping because it was against all military tradition to fire on someone carrying a white flag; being told this put their minds at ease. As they approached, several soldiers with an officer leading the way, rode out to meet them. "I am Lt. Newman, and you are?" Richard replied, "I am Lt. Roach and this is Lt. Shields." The lieutenant could not seem to take his eyes off Bubba. "What is the purpose of this white flag? Surely you're not foolish enough to think that we'll surrender to a smaller force?" Lt. Newman asked; then not waiting for a reply, continued. "If you had a superior force, most of us would be dead by now and you would not have allowed us time to regroup." Richard replied, "My commander has graciously offered to allow you to remove your dead and wounded from the road without fear of being fired upon." Lt. Newman responded, "That's very gracious indeed, Lieutenant, perhaps before this day's end we'll be able to return the favor; tell your commander that we accept his offer." Turning his attention back to Bubba he said, "I must admit that I've been attempting to maintain my composure, but I'm afraid my curiosity has gotten the better of me. May I ask why a black man is wearing the uniform of a Confederate Officer and firing on the very soldiers who have come to free his people?" Bubba carefully considered his answer before replying, "Lt. Newman, this may be hard for you to understand, but this is our home, too. The problems that exist, at least here in Folsom, will be worked out among ourselves. We choose not to accept your version of freedom for us, which we feel will only lead to a different form of slavery." "Well, in that case,

237

Lt. Shields, you and your men can prepare to die right alongside the white soldiers." Lt. Newman then saluted them saying, "Gentlemen, until we meet again on the field of battle."

As they started back Richard said, "While the lieutenant was preoccupied with you, Bubba, I had a chance to make an important observation; the insignia on the uniforms of the men accompanying the lieutenant told me that they belong to an artillery unit. That's the one thing we didn't factor in when we were making our plans; that could turn out to be a very foolish and costly mistake. They must have had their artillery pieces hidden in the covered wagons, because even our scouts didn't detect them; we've got to report this information to Bill at once." Immediately upon returning, they located Bill and informed him of the situation. "Well, gentlemen, this certainly changes things. We must leave this position at once; have the men fall back to a position closer to our camp. I'm positive the Yankees will start shelling us as soon as they've removed their wounded. They will then attack, thinking that we've been severely weakened by their shelling. We'll wait until they've entered the woods to finish us off, to launch our counter attack. Their artillery will be rendered useless at that point because they would have to fire on their own men in order to get at us. This will be a close combat, gentleman, so see to it that the men have fixed bayonets.

Now let's get the hell out of here while we're all still in one piece."

The men hastily moved to their new positions, and after making sure that things were as they should be, Bill ordered complete silence; now all they could do was wait. They didn't have to wait long. The woods seemed to come alive with thunder, as barrage after barrage fell upon the positions that they had just abandoned, and exploding shrapnel sent hot metal scattering in every direction. Bill quietly thanked Lt. Roach again, because if it had not been for his alertness, most of the men would have been killed or severely wounded in this onslaught of canon fire. They waited patiently until the shelling finally stopped, and prayed that the Yankees would overconfidently enter the woods, thinking most of them were dead. As if on cue, the Yankees did exactly that. Bubba grabbed Bill by the arm, saying, "May God be with us both today, brother," and Bill replied, "If it's my day to die, and yours, too, I'll save you a seat beside me in heaven." Bubba mutely nodded his head.

Bill looked around at his men, thinking, what an honor it is to be among them; especially these black men, who are yet slaves, and chose to fight for the men who enslave them, and the families and the land that they love so unconditionally. What courage it must take to stake their very lives on a dream, and what attachment they must have for this place they call home. Bill looked at Bubba once more, as if he might be seeing him for the last time. Clearing his throat, he gave the order; "Charge!"

The men went running towards the enemy, firing their weapons and reloading along the way. The enemy was caught totally off guard but still managed to return fire; however, the speed at which they were being attacked did not give their men on the front line enough time to reload, which meant they had to resort to hand-to-hand fighting. It was a sight to see. They were relentless and used the bayonet like they were born to it. Some of the men were wounded and covered in blood, but they still fought on. Richard was fighting brilliantly, leading his men forward without any regard for his own safety. He saw Bill rallying his men to reach a clearing in the woods; the fighting was much heavier there. Suddenly, through the clearing, he noticed a Yankee officer seated on a beautiful black stallion, riding as if in slow motion, toward Bill. As he approached Bill he raised his sword, which glimmered in the sunlight. The scene reminded him of the dream Bubba had spoken of that frequently plagued Bill, but this man was no Angel of Death, it was Lt. Newman, bent on revenge. Richard called out to Bill, who would have no time to react to the imminent danger. In moments, Bill would be at the mercy of Lt. Newman, riding with single-minded fervor. Richard quickly yelled to

Bubba, who was nearby, pointing and calling Bill's name. Even with the confusion and noise of the battle raging around him, Bubba somehow miraculously heard Bill's name being called, saw Richard pointing, and turned to look. Bubba was horrified at what he saw, thinking, good Lord, the man looks like Bill's Angel of Death! In a flash, Bubba raised his rifle, took careful aim, and with an unimaginable stroke of luck, fired one shot. Just as Lt. Newman rode in for the kill, the bullet hit him right between the eyes. Falling from his horse, his body landed almost on top of Bill, who looked at the officer lying there with the sword still in his hand, as blood spurted from the bullet hole placed neatly between his eyes. Stunned, he looked around and spotted Bubba. "No more nightmares, Bill," he shouted, "that's your Angel of Death taking his last ride!"

The fighting became more and more furious as the men pushed onward. The Yankees, seeing that there was no hope of stopping these wild men, began to hastily retreat from the woods. The men cheered as they watched them run, this was another proud moment for all of them. Bubba looked around and finally spotted Bill a few yards away, cheering with the rest of the men and he thought, Bill's plan is working, it's actually working. At that moment he heard someone shouting behind him. Lt. Roach was running towards him shouting that there were several hundred Yankee soldiers marching down the other end of the main road and that they would be attacking soon from the rear. Bubba thought, oh my God, something has gone terribly wrong! Bill had made his way to Bubba's side and after being informed of the situation, said, "Standing our ground would mean the death of all of us. Our only options are to try and fight our way past the lesser force and retreat back to the plantation, or surrender. We must decide quickly, because the only thing right now in our favor is that the Yankees we're fighting don't realize that reinforcements are on the way. We are in a "damned if you do" and "damned if you don't" situation." Lt. Roach immediately spoke up. "Surrendering is not an option, Captain, because our black soldiers would never survive in a Northern prison, they would be despised for having fought against the Yankee soldiers that came to free them. Our only hope is to retreat back to the plantation. If we succeed, the Yankees will need to regroup and come up with their plan of attack; that would buy us enough time to come up with our own plan to save the lives of the men who survive this battle." Bill agreed. "Lt. Roach has summed up our dilemma; we don't have the luxury of standing here debating this, we must act now."

The men had gathered around anxiously, as Bill issued orders. "Sgt. Kimbro, get the men into formation; we must run right through those Yankees. I don't think they have enough fight left in them. Let's hope they keep retreating so that we can get to the wagons and horses and make it back to the plantation." Bill looked at these valiant men. "You have nothing to be ashamed of this day. You have fought gallantly, but the tide has turned in favor of the Yankees. Our only hope of survival is to fight our way back to the plantation and hold them off long enough for most of you to escape with your families. Do you men have enough fight left in you to whip the hell out of those Yankees standing between you and home?" The men voiced a resounding, "Yes, sir." Bubba took a brief look around, knowing that most of these men would be dead before the day ended. His heart ached as he looked Bill straight in the eye and yelled, "Let's get the hell out of here! Let's go home!"

CHAPTER EIGHTEEN

While sitting on his porch enjoying the morning sun, Bubba reflected on the past. It's been almost thirty years since the war ended, and I'm still filled with grief for the men left on the battlefield that day long ago. He remembered how, after successfully retreating to the plantation, Bill convinced him to take the money and necessary papers and lead the surviving black soldiers and their families North, to promised safety and freedom. Bill and the remaining white soldiers would put up only a token fight in order to buy enough time for Bubba and his men to make their escape dressed as slaves; after which he would surrender. They made a pact to return after the war ended, and rebuild what would be left of their beloved home. Leaving Bill to stand alone was the hardest thing he had ever done, but in his heart he knew that Bill was right, the safety of the men that survived and their loved ones had to come first. The trip North was indeed very dangerous and difficult to endure;

that would be a story worth telling someday. His friends and both brothers, who perished that day, would always have a special place of honor in his heart. Even though the courageous black soldiers were criticized and ridiculed for their part in the war - by both newspapers and the general public - Bubba knew that they did not die in vain. What was saddest of all was that you'd be hard put to find any school that even mentioned these brave men in their history books. It seemed like most people, black and white alike, just wanted the memory of them to fade away, as if they never even existed. Right or wrong in the eyes of others, those men had the courage to stand up and fight for their beliefs and what they held most dear in their hearts. Anyone with a grain of empathy should respect that. Bubba felt tears pricking his eyes. Oh, yes, he would continue to keep the promise made to them long ago; any person in the community that had a desire for education would have that opportunity. This fervent vow was never more in evidence than it was on this magnificent day of dreams come true.

Thoughts of the past were interrupted when his daughter, Barbara, visiting with him and Hattie, said, "Mama says for you to come on and get dressed, it's getting close to the time for us to leave." "You tell Hattie that I'm on my way. I want to take one more look at this plaque, first." He reached down beside him, picked it up and began to read each inscribed name. He smiled when he saw that his daddy's name topped the list of the men who had died so courageously long ago. But as he continued to read, his smile soon gave way to tears. Calling the names aloud as if they were in formation at roll call, he said, "David, Jab, Richard, Meatball, Sammy, Arthur, Otto, Leo." Bubba could not go on. Wiping away his tears, he stood up straight and saluted them all. Then, very gently, he set down the plaque, and went inside to get dressed. A few minutes later he said to Hattie, "That man better be on time. It seems that since he's gotten old, I have to constantly remind him to be on time for everything." Hattie teased her still handsome husband, "Bubba, I guess that makes you old, too. Besides, you know how your brother is, so just stop your fussing." Just then a knock came at the door and Barbara rushed to open it, hoping it was her Uncle Bill, whom she loved dearly. Standing there, grinning from ear to ear, was Bill. "And how's my beautiful niece today?" he asked, giving her a big hug. "I'm fine, Uncle Bill; it's so good to see you, but where's Aunt Mona?" "She's right there waiting in the carriage. That woman hasn't let me get too far out of her sight since the day we got married. Now, where is that brother of mine? You know, the one who's gotten to be so fussy in his old age?" "I'm right here," Bubba said, walking into the room, "Trying to get over the shock of you being on time for a change." "Its true that I may be late for a lot of things, Bubba, but this is definitely not one of those times. If everyone is ready, we can leave right now."

The family climbed into Bill's carriage, greeting Mona warmly. Bubba carefully placed the plaque on the front seat as Bill said, "This is a fine day brother, moving your school out of those renovated cabins and erecting a new building in Folsom in memory of our comrades lost in battle. What a wonderful tribute to them; they would be very proud." Bubba only nodded, as fresh tears brimmed. He finally managed to say, a catch in his voice, "Do you ever think about what it would be like now if the South had won the war?" "Yes, I do, Bubba." "I would like to say that those inspired dreams we had as young men would have long since been realized, but the truth is you'd probably still be pickin cotton, and I'd be the Mayor of Folsom, right now." Eyes meeting, Bill and Bubba had a good, long laugh. The brothers always did enjoy a joke together. That never changed and never would.

THE END

Printed in the United States
20442LVS00001B/253-315